H5's docking bays opened and the ten shuttles of A Group spun off into space, forming the traditional V with Broadsword flying point.

Broadsword kept his eyes on the monitors as A Group swept up on *Armada*, his mind burning with the memory of the atrocity at Mare Moscoviense. He was an avenging angel, yearning for blood.

The flight plan was simple—they would sweep around the Moon and come up on *Armada* from behind, as Broadsword had done weeks earlier. It would be the most widely observed battle in history. All telescopes on H5 and all of the shuttles were watching the assault on the gigantic alien warship. And the attack, being beamed to Earth, would be seen by hundreds of millions of viewers.

What wasn't seen was the quiet departure of ten Boomerangs from the far side of *Armada*. With all eyes focused on Broadsword's attack group, the alien fighters flew swiftly away and banked off silently toward Earth. . . .

Fawcett Gold Medal Books
by Michael Jahn:

ARMADA   14388 $2.25

KINGSLEY'S EMPIRE   14324 $2.50

THE OLYMPIAN STRAIN   14342 $1.95

THE INVISIBLE MAN   P3460 $1.25

ARMADA

Michael Jahn

FAWCETT GOLD MEDAL • NEW YORK

ARMADA

Copyright © 1981 Michael Jahn

Published by Fawcett Gold Medal Books, a unit of CBS Publications, the Consumer Publishing Division of CBS Inc.

ISBN: 0-449-14388-0

Printed in the United States of America

First Fawcett Gold Medal printing: February 1981

10 9 8 7 6 5 4 3 2 1

For Evergreen

ARMADA

ONE

The rock was the size of a small car. It came from the outer fringes of the solar system, following the path of Comet J1995 which had passed by a month earlier and a little more than a million miles closer to the sun. The rock caught the sunlight and reflected it in a strong metallic glint which inflamed Broadsword's spirit of adventure. "Hold on," he said, reaching for the throttles.

Margot covered his hand and the throttle levers with hers.

"You'll make us late," she said.

"So what?"

"H5 needs the cargo."

"What? More crystals for more transistors so everyone can have *two* wrist radios?"

Margot smiled at her captain with true affection.

"It's your funeral, Adonis," she said, jamming his hand, and the throttles, forward.

The *Ark Royal* leaped forward as if it had been kicked in the behind. The huge Multi-Burn Engines—the principal advantage of the series 500 shuttles—sent three plumes of flame searing into the darkness of interplanetary space. Broadsword let out a whoop of joy as he felt the spacecraft tremble. He loved the new shuttles. You could feel the power, feel the whole craft shake, and thrill to the rumble of the engines. Real flying had come to space, and he couldn't get enough of it.

Broadsword put the *Ark Royal* into a sweeping turn to starboard and up. While Margot punched instructions into the target computer, he craned his neck to peer out the cockpit window, looking for the asteroid.

"Where'd it go?" he asked.

Numbers flashed on one of the two dozen monitors set into the walls, ceiling and dashboard of the cockpit.

"Your rock is at 337.42 by 57.29," she replied. "If you want I can punch it into navigation."

"I want you to show me where it is," he snapped.

Margot sighed and joined him in squinting out the window.

"Right there," she said, pointing at a spot in the starfield about five thousand miles from Earth.

"I don't see it."

"One o'clock low. You're too high. Why don't you let the computer fly her?"

"I've warned you about that attitude," Broadsword snapped. "Okay...I see it."

"I read it traveling at a shade over thirty-four thousand miles an hour, and it's got four miles on us."

"Not for long."

He brought the nose down and swung the ship a bit to starboard. Broadsword inched the throttles a bit further forward. The *Ark Royal*'s trembling took on a different tempo as the distance closed.

"Fire up a Rock Buster," he said.

"You can't waste another missile," his copilot warned. "You're in for it with Edwards now." She looked at Broadsword for a reaction, but got none. His black eyes were set on the asteroid he was chasing, his light red skin shining in the light reflected from the gigantic blue-and-white marble that was Earth. Nobody should be allowed to be that good-looking, Margot thought, especially at age twenty-four.

"Okay," she sighed, "we can say the rock was going to hit the atmosphere."

"And impact over New York," he replied. "I knew I could rely on you."

Margot flipped open the safety panel covering the missile-arming mechanism. The *Ark Royal*, like all the ten shuttles working between the Earth, Moon and H5, carried half-a-dozen small missiles officially designated Bloodhounds but universally known among the pilots as Rock Busters. They were for occasional use in asteroid destruction or in the elimination of some of the twelve thousand pieces of space junk orbiting Earth. Margot fed the coordinates of the asteroid, now only a half mile away, into the fire control computer.

"Armed and ready," she said.

Broadsword fingered the red button atop his control stick nervously and watched as the asteroid, its image magnified electronically, drifted under the cross hairs of the target monitor.

"It seems a shame to waste it," he said. "I'd rather pick it up and give it to Curtiss. He could

11

probably get a good price for it. There may be some gold in there, you never know."

"We have a full cargo bay."

"I could eighty-six the cargo," he said.

Margot groaned. "Fire the goddam thing and let's go," she said.

Broadsword grinned and pressed the button. There was a flash of light as the thin, silver missile streaked from its wing launcher and disappeared into the void ahead. Seconds later, a brilliant flash of fire lit up the darkness. Despite herself, Margot clapped her hands in delight.

"Beautiful! Right on the nose!"

Broadsword gave her knee a friendly sort of squeeze. "That's more like it," he said. "I was afraid you were turning serious on me."

"Sorry," she replied, closing the missile-arming panel. "I'm still a little hung over from last night."

"I'll make you a Bloody Mary when we get to H5," Broadsword said.

"Don't. You're lousy at it. Let me fly her, would you? You've had your turn."

Broadsword shrugged and turned the controls over to her. She put the *Ark Royal* into a sweeping turn to port and aimed her in the direction of the gigantic space station spinning in orbit between the Earth and the Moon. Broadsword undid his safety belts, bent his legs and propelled himself backwards out of his seat. He spun twice in the air, his legs tucked under, then executed a perfect headfirst dive into the access tube leading to the lower level.

"You're gonna break your fuckin' neck doing that some day," Margot shouted, to which he replied, "Jealousy is unbecoming."

When Broadsword reappeared, he carried two plastic tubes filled with liquid.

"Firewater?" she asked.

He nodded. "Moulin-à-Vent, '89."

"You're kidding."

"Yeah. I got you some cheap Napa Valley brandy. That should take care of your hangover."

"What have you got?"

"Iced tea."

"Child," she retorted, with a gentle sort of scorn.

He climbed back into his seat without bothering to buckle up and squeezed some of the tea into his throat. It cooled him, but went down only with difficulty in the weightlessness of space, and he longed then for the simulated gravity of H5. Margot drank with him, and as the two-hundred-thousand-pound spacecraft sped away from Earth at better than forty thousand miles an hour, Broadsword closed his eyes and let the silence of coasting in space sweep over him. The engines were off. There would be no sound other than their own until it was time to fire the retros, and that wouldn't be for a while.

Broadsword finished his drink and tossed the tube aimlessly over his shoulder without opening his eyes, unaware that Margot was watching him. Eyes closed, he thought about his life. Being the first Native American in space was enough accomplishment; Broadsword had become NASA's top pilot, and both he and Margot were celebrities back on Earth. Part of the reason for his fame was his looks. He knew he was impossibly good-looking. It was something Margot taunted him about without end. Being an American Indian was fashionable, and having the reputation of being a rogue didn't hurt, either. He didn't think of himself as being a rogue. He knew he was fun-loving, something he shared with Margot. Coming as they did on the heels of decades of Boy Scout astronauts, it was perhaps inevitable that they would achieve notoriety. Sometimes Broadsword wondered if he loved Margot. But she was ten years older than he, which seemed like a lot, and it was, after all, safer just having fun with her.

His musing was cut short by a blast from the radio.

"*Ark Royal,* this is H5 Control, do you copy?"

"Oh, shit," he said out loud.

Margot laughed. "You knew it was coming."

"Yeah, but so fast? I was hoping to get some sleep."

The radio spoke again, repeating its message. The voice was soft, feminine and familiar.

"*Ark Royal,* this is H5 Control, please respond."

"Answer her, lover," Margot said. "Yon Juliet beckons, and you doth remain silent."

"Kiss my ass," Broadsword said, with some emotion. The voice belonged to Leslie Dixon, the chief radio operator for H5, a 19-year-old girl on her first tour of duty in space who was Broadsword's latest flame. His attraction to her amused Margot; Leslie was just a teenager. Correspondingly, Broadsword was embarrassed that for the first time Margot had something to beat him over the head with. "Kiss my ass," he said again.

"You bare it, baby, and I'll kiss it," Margot shot back, picking up the radio headset and putting it on. The cheap Napa Valley brandy was doing its job.

"H5 Control," she radioed, "this is *Ark Royal.*"

Leslie seemed disappointed, and turned official.

"*Ark Royal*, why are you 4,287 miles off course, and why did you fire a Bloodhound missile?"

"You've been snooping, H5 Control," Margot replied. "We are off course due to the necessity of intercepting a large asteroid which was within an hour of entering the atmosphere, projected impact point the northeast United States. The same explanation holds for the use of the Rock Buster. Anything else you want to know?"

"Jesus Christ," Broadsword breathed.

The radio remained silent for a moment, then Leslie returned.

"*Ark Royal*, thanks for the information; are you still capable of landing on schedule?"

"Of course," Margot said.

"Very good. Land docking bay 7, and please ask Captain Broadsword to try not to wreck the bay this time."

Margot confirmed receipt of the message and took off her headset.

"It sounds like love to me," she said, with a laugh.

TWO

Habitat Five was a gigantic silver inner tube, more than a mile across and four miles around, with five spokes leading to a central hub. It was visible from the Earth as a bright star and from the Moon as a gleaming ring amid the splendor of the starfield. Broadsword approached it slowly. The docking bays were on the spokes and rotated with the same motion that allowed artificial gravity in the ring. But it meant that he'd have to fly sideways as well as up if he meant to fit the spacecraft into the bay without smashing things as he'd done often enough in the past. The month before, he'd bent an air lock and, before that, twisted one of the grappling arms.

It wasn't that Broadsword *meant* to wreck H5. The NaviComputer was capable of taking the *Ark Royal* in for a perfect landing. But being the fleet's top pilot was a heavy burden, and Broadsword meant to protect his reputation by learning to dock properly. Of course, the Council long ago had recognized his shortcoming and forbade him to dock manually. He ignored the instruction. He knew he'd get it right eventually.

Broadsword cruised in slowly over the central hub of H5. Spherical and cut in halves like a grapefruit, with the spokes leading to the ring joined in the center, the hub had maneuvering jets with which to maintain counterspin. While the ring spun at a rate of one revolution per minute to maintain gravity, the hub was motionless in space. In its weightlessness, manufacturing operations impossible on Earth or Moon were maintained. It was for those operations that the *Ark Royal*'s cargo was destined. Once the shuttle was fitted into the docking bay which matched perfectly the upper hemisphere of the craft, the bay would be pressurized and, while the cargo was being extracted, Nathaniel Broadsword and Margot Chambers would trot off to the ring to get drunk and raise hell. That was how it usually worked.

As he passed the partially finished lower half of the hub, Broadsword heard the radio crackle as Leslie Dixon's voice sounded again.

"*Ark Royal,* this is H5 Control, we're not receiving your computer tie-in."

"They got you this time," Margot said.

"Not a chance," Broadsword replied, putting on his headset and flicking it into life. "H5 Control, *Ark Royal* here, landing manually."

For the first time, Leslie's voice lost its professional cool. "No way! You know you've been told not to! If you try it and..."

Broadsword cut her off. "Sorry, H5 Control, but we're having computer problems. I can't trust the automatic pilot this time. It damn near killed us when we were chasing that rock. I'll dock the ship myself. Pilot's prerogative."

Margot whistled admiringly. "You got one of the sweetest lines of bullshit I ever heard," she said.

"Thank you, darling," Broadsword replied, switching the stick control from main engines to maneuvering jets.

"Try not to wreck the place just the same," she said, bracing herself.

Leslie was back on the radio. "Be careful, Nathaniel," she said.

Margot mimicked her. "'Be careful, Nathaniel.' How sweet. Why don't you marry her?"

"Maybe I will."

"Do I get to go to the wedding?"

"Sure. You'd make a great best man."

Margot bristled and shook a menacing fist at him. "That was a low blow, Broadsword, even for you."

"Be quiet," he replied, smiling. "I have to concentrate."

Working the stick, he maneuvered the spacecraft under the spoke containing bay 7. The open doors revealed an interior contoured to the shape of the shuttle. Broadsword brought the *Ark Royal* under it and started up, trying to swing the craft vertically and horizontally at the same time. Margot shook her head in despair as the *Ark Royal* hit the grappling arms just a bit too hard, snapping one of them clean off. Almost immediately, the radio spoke.

"*Ark Royal*, this is bay 7, we have a problem. Please shut down all propulsion systems and stand by."

"You did it again," Margot said, shutting off the engines.

"It kinds of looks that way," Broadsword said, climbing out of his seat and up what used to be the cockpit floor until he got to the access tube. Docked as they were halfway up an H5 spoke, there was partial gravity in the *Ark Royal*. Broadsword waited at the exit hatch while Margot finished her postflight chores and the bay 7 attendants replaced the broken grappling arm, secured the ship into the bay and pressurized it. A short time later they were riding the elevator to the ring.

"I'm going to take a shower and change my clothes," Margot said. "Meet me in a half hour."

"Make it an hour," he replied.

"Oh, are we going to visit the fair Leslie?"

"And why not? I don't get anything from you but abuse."

She turned to him, wrapped her arms around his neck and kissed him playfully on the lips. "You need but ask," she said.

"I don't like older women," he said.

"I'm thirty-four," she protested.

"And over the hill."

Actually, Margot Chambers was anything but that. She had reddish blond hair and was tall with large breasts and a swaggering attitude that would appear threatening to a lesser man. Many men *were* frightened of her, but Broadsword thought she was fun. Were he not addicted to short blondes like Leslie Dixon, there might have been a chance for them.

"You're a goddam dumb Indian, you know

that?" she said. "I wonder how you ever made captain."

"I wonder why you never did."

"I like flying with you," she said. "Particularly when you take the blame for busting up the docking bays."

The elevator ground to a halt, and the doors opened. Leslie was standing there, and looked with disapproval as Margot uncoiled her arms from around Broadsword's neck.

"Good afternoon, Leslie," Margot said, unable to suppress a slight grin.

Leslie was less enthusiastic. "Hello, Margot," she said, rather bleakly.

Margot swept away and down the hall in the direction of the living quarters. "See you in an hour," she called over her shoulder.

Broadsword stepped out of the elevator and looked around at the splendor of H5. The station was only partly built. The skin was in place all around it, but the cavernous interior which one day would be home for ten thousand colonists was largely unfinished. Only one of the five sections of rim was complete, but it was magnificent. Over three-quarters of a mile long and four hundred feet high, it was a wonderful combination of terraced gardens, apartment and shopping complexes, an athletic field, and a cylindrical office and scientific tower which rose forty stories from one side of the rim to the other. At varying places along the skin of the section, pneumatic elevators led to astronomical observatories. As yet it was only sparsely inhabited; a month away from the official opening, only 250 construction workers and scientists roamed the gardens and lunched beneath shade trees planted in enriched moon soil.

Broadsword ran his fingers over the branches of a carefully tended azalea, smiled and turned his attention back to the girl.

"This place is almost as beautiful as you are," he said.

Leslie was only partly mollified, and answered, with a pout, "Did you tell that to Margot, too?"

"She's my copilot and friend," Broadsword replied.

"A close friend, I see."

Broadsword held her face between his hands and kissed her. "I go to Earth for three days and look what happens," he said.

She smiled then, and kissed him back. "I have to get back to work. There are three ore freighters coming in."

"Terrific," he said, without the slightest trace of interest.

"Don't knock them. At least they know how to dock. That was a real neat job you did coming in today. Edwards wants to see you. You're in trouble with him again."

"What else is new?"

"You broke another grappling arm. He won't let you get away with it this time."

"We'll see. How about dinner tonight? I was just coming down to Control to ask you."

"You're not going out with Margot?" Leslie asked.

"Just for drinks. It was a long flight. Seven o'clock? I brought a couple of really gorgeous steaks with me."

"It's a deal," she said happily, giving him another quick kiss before running off through a small, terraced park which stood between the elevators and the mammoth office and scientific tower. Broadsword watched her go, then caught the first tram to the apartment complex in which the pilots were quartered.

An hour later, he walked into the burgundy-and-black vinyl luxury of the cozy little bar which the Council had nearly spoiled by naming it The Sky Inn. Set part of the way up an outer face of the rim, one wall was entirely glass, and with the dark colors inside, the starfield made a spectacular backdrop for an evening out. Like every facility in H5, it wasn't quite open, for there were few colonists to patronize it as yet. But its location on the skin amid the astronomical observatories gave the Inn a brisk trade among the star watchers, and at any time it was impossible not to hear an argument on one or another aspect of cosmic research. In recognition of this, the management had bought and transported to H5 a brass Victorian refractor and mounted it next to the bar for customers to use in settling arguments or amusing themselves.

Margot stood with her back to the bar, both elbows resting upon it, holding a drink. While she wore the standard issue blue jump suit, she had buckled a broad, filagreed silver belt around it. Broadsword wore faded jeans with a Western shirt, a tweed sports jacket and cowboy boots featuring stitched pictures of various cacti.

"You're late," she said, handing him a drink.

"What's this?"

"A *Virgin* Mary," she replied. "Pointless, if you ask me. I thought Indians drank."

"Not this one," Broadsword answered, taking a sip and nodding appreciatively. "This isn't bad ... for a woman."

"Don't push your luck, Broadsword. Little Big Horn is just history now."

"Sitting Bull was a Sioux. I'm a Mohawk."

"You're lots of things, including a child. What are you dressed up for? Got a date tonight?"

He nodded. "I'm cooking dinner for Leslie ... the steaks I bought at Kennedy."

"God help her. I've tasted your cooking. Did Edwards get to you yet, speaking of disasters?"

Broadsword joined her in leaning against the bar. They couldn't see the stars that way, but in the seven hours' flight from Earth to H5 they'd seen more than enough.

"He left word, but I haven't gotten around to seeing him yet. I know what he's going to say, so why should I bother?"

"You realize that all that stuff we handed H5 Control about the asteroid impacting over America and the computer being out was sheer bullshit, don't you?"

"Of course, but they can't prove otherwise. Besides, Edwards can't fire me himself. It would take a majority of the Council, and he doesn't have the votes."

"He can revoke your landing rights," she said.

"Only until the next meeting of the Council. For an old woman, you don't know a hell of a lot about politics."

Margot sighed and finished her drink, setting the glass down with enough force to startle the only other patron of the bar, a middle-aged astronomer a few stools down who had been caught up in examination of some eight-by-tens.

"I got better things to do than stand here and listen to you," she said.

"Like what? I thought you were gonna do some drinking?"

"I was until you made a date to poison Lolita with your home cooking. Besides, Curtiss is in town."

"What?" Broadsword exclaimed. "I thought he was off in the Belt collecting rocks!"

"He was," she replied, pleased to see that Broadsword was pleased. "He's back. I *thought* you hadn't noticed him."

"Noticed him? When?"

"The *Columbia* was parked in docking bay 4 when we came in. You were too busy wrecking bay 7 to see her."

"You're sure it was the *Columbia?*"

"I'd recognize those rust spots anywhere."

Broadsword bolted down his drink. "Let's go find him," he said. "We have a lot to talk about. I haven't seen him for a month, and I've *never* been to the Asteroid Belt. Come on..."

He started for the door, but Margot called him back.

"*I'll* find him," she said. "My need for his company is more pressing than yours."

She unzipped her jump suit nearly to the waist, gave Broadsword a pat on the cheek and went to the door.

"I left the tab for you to pay," she said, and went.

Broadsword watched her go, then turned back to the bar, shaking his head. He ordered another

Virgin Mary and drank it while peering out at the stars, pondering his three years in space. After a time he wandered over to the old brass telescope and peered into it. Though it was pointed at the ecliptic, the plane in which most of the planets orbit, he could see little. H5's rotation made everything go past the lens too fast. He was about to return to the bar when he felt a presence at his side.

It was the astronomer who had been poring over the eight-by-tens. An agreeable-looking, small man in his early 50s, he held a green-colored drink and patted the old telescope condescendingly.

"You won't see anything with that," he said.

"I know," Broadsword replied, standing away from the instrument.

"Even if it was up-to-date, the station revolves too fast. You have to go to the weightless observatory in the hub."

"Do I know you?" Broadsword asked.

"You flew me up from Earth three weeks ago," the man said.

"Of course," Broadsword said as if he remembered, which he didn't. He flew so many scientists from Earth to the Moon to H5 and back, at times he felt like a ferry captain.

"My name is Haskins, Walter Haskins." He extended his hand, and Broadsword shook it. "Planetary astronomy, with a specialty in comets."

"Nathaniel Broadsword, shuttle pilot, with a specialty in pissing people off."

Haskins didn't seem to find that statement particularly interesting; he returned to his photographs, one of which he showed to Broadsword. It was a dense starfield, with one or two bright objects, and a small one which had made a tiny streak on the film.

"Do you see that?" Haskins asked, pointing at it.

Broadsword nodded. "An asteroid. Or a comet. So what?"

"I'm not sure what it is."

"If it's in the plane of the ecliptic, it's probably an asteroid. If not, maybe a comet."

"It's in the direction of Jupiter."

"Then it's a rock. Terrific. If it comes near us I'll blow the shit out of it."

The astronomer shook his head. "It isn't behaving like anything I know. If it's in orbit, it's the strangest one I've ever seen. Also..." the man paused, accenting the significance of his words, "I could swear it moved out of its trajectory while passing Jupiter. It just doesn't make sense."

Broadsword finished his second drink and set the glass down on the bar. Then he gave the fellow an encouraging pat on the back. "I'll put you up for the Nobel Prize when you figure out what it is," he said.

THREE

Howard Edwards was a thin, slightly stooped man of sixty, with a military crew cut that had gone white, making his head look a bit like a tennis ball. Edwards had been in the space program since the days of the Mercury astronauts, and viewed his appointment as Chairman of the Habitat Five Council as the crowning achievement of a life spent behind a desk. He fully intended to live out the rest of his life in the post, in his daydreams the Founding Father of the world's first space colony. Edwards took as an assault on his very being anything which interfered with the smooth running of H5. Nathaniel Broadsword, Margot Chambers and, to a lesser extent (because he was not often around) Curtiss Baxter were seen by him as enemies. He liked team players, and they were anything but that.

But they were popular. Broadsword and Chambers were glamorous figures back on Earth, and Baxter held the respect of nearly all aboard H5 and the various scientific and mining bases on the

Moon. Try as he might to rid himself of these anomalies in his neatly ordered world, Edwards was unable to do it.

When Broadsword stepped into his office on the top floor of the Tower, Edwards was bent over a stack of vouchers, signing some, putting others aside. Broadsword, sensing he was being deliberately ignored, walked up to the desk and stood there, idly twirling his tennis racket. He was dressed for a match and sported his new graphite racket with great pride. After a moment, Edwards looked up.

"What are you dressed for?" he asked.

"It's not obvious?"

"Of course it's obvious. That was a rhetorical question. What I meant is, why aren't you dressed for a flight?"

"Because I'm playing tennis, not flying. This is my day off. I came to see you because Leslie said you wanted to talk to me. If you'd like to put it off until tomorrow..."

"No," Edwards said quickly. "This will be fine. Sit down, Captain."

"No thank you, I'd rather stand. Bailey is waiting on the courts."

"Bailey?"

"Flies the *Lexington*."

"Oh, *that* Bailey. Well, have a nice match. Look, Broadsword, I'll come right to the point. H5 is a month away from opening day ceremonies. There will be a lot of dignitaries up here, and a lot of press. You'll be ferrying many of them yourself. This sector is now a showplace... ready for colonization. If we're going to attract colonists to this station, everything has to be in tip-top shape. *In-*

cluding the docking bays! Do I make myself clear?"

"Quite."

"We can't have you coming in with half-a-dozen reporters from the *New York Times* aboard if you're going to fly the *Ark Royal* through the wall."

Broadsword, feeling chastised, looked down at the floor.

"In the future, you will let the NaviComputer do the docking. You're a good pilot, Broadsword, but you must face the fact that docking is not one of your talents."

"Yes, sir."

"Neither is lying," Edwards said. "We tracked that 'rock' you saw fit to blow out of the sky. We didn't find any pressing need either to pursue it or destroy it. Bloodhound missiles are not cheap, and neither is fuel for running the MBEs at full throttle."

"I guess not," Broadsword said.

"You seem to have a personal need to fancy yourself a fighter pilot. When I was a boy, Captain, we had something called World War II in which it was very glamorous to fly around shooting at things. It was also very necessary. That necessity no longer exists. You are a shuttle pilot... in effect, a ferry captain. It's not too romantic, but try to think of it that way."

Broadsword nodded.

"There's something else you can do for me," Edwards said.

"What's that?" Broadsword asked, seeing a way to put himself back in Edwards' good graces.

"Do you know Walter Haskins?"

"Unh...planetary astronomer, specialty in comets? I met him at the Inn yesterday."

"That's him. He has spotted this peculiar object out in the vicinity of Jupiter which he can't identify."

"So I hear."

"Well, Haskins is a full professor at Columbia University, several of whose trustees carry much weight with the Council. Haskins doesn't feel the weightless observatory at the hub is good enough for him. He wants to take the twenty-inch reflector a few hundred yards out and run a few spectra on his mysterious object. Would you fly the mission for him?"

"When?" Broadsword asked.

"This afternoon. I know it's your day off, but he only needs half an hour observation time, which means the whole thing will only take you a little more than an hour. You do it, Broadsword, and I'll forget about the grappling arm you broke yesterday."

Broadsword started to object.

"*And* wasting the Bloodhound missile," Edwards added.

"All right," Broadsword said reluctantly.

"Good. The telescope is being loaded aboard the *Ark Royal* at this moment. Be on board at 3 P.M."

"Will I need Margot?"

"Not for this one. You can handle it yourself. As long..."

"I know," Broadsword cut in. "As long as I let the NaviComputer do the docking."

The *Ark Royal* sat quietly in space five miles to the outbound side of H5. The cargo bay doors vere open, and the Cassegrain Observation Segment filled the same cargo space that a day before held several tons of the raw materials with which to grow crystals for electronic components. The telescope itself was in an unpressurized section of the bay. Haskins stood in the pressurized experiment segment, working the controls and watching the images as they appeared on his computer screen. Bored half to death, Broadsword lay motionless in midair nearby, trying to make himself sneeze to see if the force would start him spinning.

Haskins was enthralled with the image of a spectrum on his screen. "You see?" he asked.

"Sure," Broadsword said. "What does it mean?"

"It means that I still don't know what the object is."

"It's not an asteroid?"

"Nor a comet. Nor anything I'm familiar with. For one thing, look at this positional shift."

Haskins punched up a split image showing a distinct shift in the object's position.

"Between 4 P.M. yesterday and 4 P.M. today, it traveled twenty million miles. That means an approximate velocity of over eight hundred thousand miles per hour."

Broadsword looked over at the man. "There must be something wrong with your math. Nothing in this solar system goes that fast."

"Other than light," Haskins said. "You're right, Captain, but I assure you there's nothing wrong with my computations. Furthermore, the object quite definitely *did* swerve toward Jupiter as it passed that planet."

Unable to get himself to sneeze, Broadsword grabbed hold of a bulkhead and pulled himself into the travel tube connecting the experiment segment with the crew's quarters. After a second, he rolled over and lay in the tube, resting his chin on his hands and looking at the scientist.

"A fault in the computer?" he asked.

"I don't think so, but I plan to check it."

"Well, Doctor," Broadsword said, "I'm gonna go get up a head of steam, if you don't mind."

"That's fine. I'm all done here. If you have the time, I'd like to do it again tomorrow."

Broadsword shrugged. "I have to fly a mining crew to the Moon and return with a load of ore, but that's only in the morning. I wouldn't mind coming out here for another little nap in the afternoon. I must say, of all the astronomers I've taken into orbit and beyond, you cause the least trouble."

"Thank you," Haskins replied.

"Besides, I admire a man who has the nerve to admit it when he doesn't know what the hell something is."

Haskins laughed. "Well put," he said. "You know, this mysterious object of mine could turn out to be fairly important. If so, they might put our names on it, like with Halley's Comet?"

"They might put *your* name on it," Broadsword replied, "as in 'Haskins' Mysterious Object.' But I'm certain they won't stick the thing with a 'Broadsword.' You're the discoverer of it, whatever it turns out to be. I'm just the ferry captain."

"You're too modest, Captain," Haskins said. It made no difference. Broadsword was back in the captain's seat, warming up the MBEs.

When Haskins returned to the cabin with his data, Broadsword closed the cargo bay and took the *Ark Royal* back to H5. Dutifully letting the

NaviComputer dock the ship, he watched while the longshoremen removed the Cassegrain Observation Segment, clearing the cargo bay for the next day's shipment of ore. Then he rode the elevator to the rim. It was nearly six in the evening, and the automatic nighttime had already adjusted the light reaching the outdoor areas of the sector to approximate that in the central United States at the same hour.

Broadsword had some time before he was to meet Leslie, so he decided a cool drink was in order. He made his way to the Sky Inn, and walked straight into the arms of Curtiss Baxter.

"Come on in, boy," Baxter growled, his Kentucky accent snapping vowels around as if they were baseballs. "I'm in a good mood, and I'm buyin'."

FOUR

A fearlessly deliberate grin appeared on Broadsword's face, and he squeezed Baxter's arms. "You're still alive, you son of a bitch."

"Of course I'm still alive. You don't think a bunch of rocks can kill me, do you?"

The two men went into the bar, where a tankard of ale and a bottle of quinine soon appeared.

"Margot saw the *Columbia* when we docked yesterday. I was busy at the time."

"So I heard," Baxter said, with a laugh. "How'd you and Edwards get along afterwards?"

"I got off easy," Broadsword replied. "A mild tongue-lashing. And I have to fly this crazy astronomer around for a day or two."

"*All* astronomers are crazy. What about that bunch down in Puerto Rico who've spent the last twenty years sending love letters to all the little green men in the galaxy? Nobody's sent nothin' back yet."

Broadsword nodded. "This guy's found something he says is heading this way at eight hundred thousand miles an hour. Not only that, but it took a side trip to have a peek at Jupiter."

"Great," Baxter said. "If he figures out how it does it, I'll buy the patent. I could have used a couple new engines on my way to the Belt and back. Christ, what a long haul!"

Broadsword took a mouthful of tonic, savored it for a second, then swallowed.

"Did you make money on the trip?" he asked.

"Yeah. I'm not gettin' rich or anything, but I'm payin' the bills. I brought back a cargo bay full of ore and two barges. The clowns in Fabrication gave me enough for the load to keep the wolves from the door for a couple of months."

"That's great," Broadsword said. He liked Baxter; saw him, in fact, as a kind of father. Baxter was fifty-two and had a sort of charm not often seen among the space travelers of 1995. He was an independent asteroid and Moon prospector who owned his own shuttle—the original *Columbia*, the first shuttle to fly into space, back in 1981. He had bought it from NASA once the series 200 shuttles came in, and upgraded it, only recently adding three new Multi-Burn Engines to the rubber band and paper clip mechanics of his craft. Working on his own, he mined the Moon and the Asteroid Belt for minerals which he sold to the manufacturing arm of H5. Baxter was fiercely independent, hateful of Earth,. which he had long abandoned, and proud of being both the first independent space entrepeneur and the first man to leave Earth forever. He hadn't set foot on the planet in a decade and, in fact, couldn't. Having the only private space vehicle, he couldn't land on Earth as NASA wouldn't spend the money to fire him back into space, and the cost of fuel for an Earth departure was way beyond his means.

"So what have you been up to, boy?" Baxter asked.

"Aside from banging up the docking bays, not a hell of a lot. I just came up from the Cape yesterday, blew the shit out of an asteroid on the way, had a date with Leslie, got chewed out by Edwards and played some tennis."

"You lead one excitin' life," Baxter said. "Tell me about the Belt. What was it like?"

"About as excitin' as your life. Those rocks are a good distance apart, you know. If you weren't lookin' for 'em, you'd never know you were there. But I got some good stuff. Some really good stuff. You never know what the hell you're gonna find floating around in space. I got half a mind to go after a comet the next time one comes 'round. This crazy astronomer of yours—is there any chance that would be a new comet he's discovered?"

"He says not."

"Well, that would be just my luck. I'm gonna have to go pokin' back around my Moon claim."

"At Eichstadt?" Broadsword asked. "Do you still expect to find something there?"

"Sure I do. And I will too, soon as I get a little rest and recreation."

"While we're on the subject of recreation, where's my copilot? I haven't seen or heard from her all day."

"Shopping, I think. She had something she wanted to buy. Anyway, what she and I do is none of your business. You're too young for such things."

"Mmmf," Broadsword said.

"I don't want to sound like I'm bein' hospitable,"

39

Baxter went on, "but I was thinking of tossing some food together tonight at my place. Nothing fancy...some Irish stew, a little booze, and I got half a bushel of clams I mean to open up."

Broadsword was fascinated.

"How in hell did you manage to get half a bushel of clams two hundred thousand miles from Earth?" he asked.

"Trade secret, boy, but I can tell you it cost me a pretty penny."

"I can't think of anyone else in the world who could pull that off."

"You want to come or not? I got to make up the guest list."

"Who else will be there?"

"Just you, me, your copilot and that little blonde you've been chasing lately. How about it?"

"Unh...sure...why not?"

Baxter held up his mug, and Broadsword touched his bottle to it.

The staff apartments were in tiers, five flats to a tier, spaced around the public grounds among the artificial lakes, tennis courts, outdoor theaters and other facilities. Each apartment, no matter how small, had a terrace from which one could watch the Moon at night. At that distance it took up a large portion of sky. In the direction of the Earth, the bright bulk of Solar Collector One appeared as a brilliant star as it beamed the sun's energy to a station in Nebraska.

It was just before midnight when Broadsword walked onto Baxter's terrace and looked out at the sector. The park lamps glowed softly, casting shadows across the greens and giving him the impression that he was on Earth gazing out at a city park. His belly was full of clams and stew, and an old Thelonius Monk tape played softly from a wall speaker.

Inside, Margot and Leslie had put aside their differences and become engaged in a noisy discussion of the upcoming Academy Awards. Broadsword stood on the balcony until Baxter came out, a cigar in his mouth and a bottle in his hand.

"Bourbon?" he asked.

"Nope," Broadsword replied.

"You're too young to be entrusted with anything important anyway."

Broadsword turned to face him, leaning against the terrace railing. "Where'd you get the clams?" he asked.

"Bailey flew 'em up to me in the *Lexington*. They're genuine Blue Points. How'd they taste?"

"Great," Broadsword said. "How'd he get them past the longshoremen?"

"That ain't my problem, boy. Hey, I kind of like that girl of yours."

"Thanks."

"Is this serious or anything?" Baxter asked.

"I don't know," Broadsword laughed. "I've only dated her a couple of times. What do you care?"

"I worry about you. You ought to do something with your life, not just stay in your cozy job."

"Cozy job?" Broadsword exclaimed. "I'm a shuttle pilot!"

"Terrific. You fly crazy scientists to and from H5 and drunken miners to and from the Moon. Now and then you go chasing after a loose rock

41

for which you get your balls broken. Tell me how exciting your life is."

"I suppose you've got a better idea."

"You could go into business with me," Baxter said.

"You're kidding!"

"Nope. With you and me working together, we could make a trip to the Belt every few months. With that and the mining operation at Eichstadt, we'd clean up."

"Clean up what? There's no mining operation at Eichstadt, just another barren crater."

"Look, kid, South Africa wasn't any big deal before diamonds were discovered there. What do you want, Beverly Hills or a vein of gold?"

Broadsword sighed and pushed away from the railing.

"I've got to get going. I'm flying a Moon mission in the morning."

"What do you say to working with me?" Baxter asked.

"I can't quit my job," Broadsword said. "Flying is all I can do."

"You can fly for me."

"I'd only be in your way," Broadsword said. "Look, Curt, this isn't the time to talk about it. It's late, considering the hour I got to get up at tomorrow.... Besides," he added, heading for the inside of the apartment, "I'm too young to be entrusted with anything important."

Broadsword went inside and collected Leslie. It had been a successful evening, even if the offer of a new lifestyle was a bit unexpected. They said their goodnights, then walked arm in arm to her apartment. Her studio was in a block of flats on the other side of the tennis courts from the pilots' quarters. It was light and airy, decorated with her own watercolors. He watched her as she made coffee. Leslie was short, scarcely five feet tall, with a slim body and a cherubic face framed by long, straight hair. She struck him as angelic and, to a certain extent, she was just that. Sure, she *was* the voice of H5 Control and in that capacity had to chide him a lot. But Leslie had a basic innocence which Broadsword found exciting.

She handed him a cup of espresso and sat beside him. "It's been a beautiful evening," she said. "I ate too much, though. I'll have to work it off tomorrow."

"I'm free in the evening if you want to play some tennis," he offered.

"Okay," she said, taking a sip of espresso and putting the cup down, "but I'm not really in your league."

He set his cup next to hers and coiled an arm around her shoulders. "Only one way to find out," Broadsword said, leaning into her and pressing his lips to hers. Their bodies came together. He ran his fingers lightly up and down her spine, and they didn't pull apart until both were out of breath.

Abruptly, she took his arm from around her shoulders and, leaning back against the couch, held his hand in both of hers. She sighed and closed her eyes.

"I know," Broadsword said quietly, picking up his coffee cup, "not on the fourth date."

"That was unfair," she replied.

"I guess it was." He took a sip of espresso.

"I like you, Nathaniel, but you frighten me."

"You're not serious," he laughed.

"I am. I just don't know what to make of you."

"I'm not all that complex," Broadsword said.

Leslie gestured in the air as if painting one of her watercolors, searching for words. "You're ...different...you..."

"Get in too much trouble," he said.

"That's not it...exactly...but...are you really going to quit NASA?"

Broadsword laughed. "So that's it, huh? You want a team player, with a regular income and a secure future. Well, let me assure you I have no intention of going into business with Baxter." He patted her on the knee, finished his coffee and stood. "That doesn't mean Edwards won't sack me if he gets a chance."

Leslie went to him, put her arms around his neck and kissed him again. Then she pulled away and touched her fingertips to his cheek. "God, you're beautiful," she said.

"You ain't so bad yourself, kid," Broadsword replied, giving her a pat on the ass and going to the door.

FIVE

Broadsword had come to the conclusion that sneezing probably wasn't enough to start his body spinning in weightlessness. Besides, in the sterile atmosphere of the Cassegrain Observation Segment, there was no dust and certainly no pollen to start a sneeze going. Broadsword abandoned all hope of completing his experiment and, with a slight push on a bulkhead, propelled himself over to where Haskins stood twiddling with the telescope controls.

"Finished?" he asked.

"Yes," the scientist replied, a bit breathlessly.

"Find anything new?"

"I have a better picture of it," Haskins said, touching a series of buttons until an image appeared on the screen. It showed the object, brilliant against the starfield but still appearing as a speck of light.

"I can't see any form to it," Broadsword said.

"It's too early for that yet. Too early for a tail, too, if it's a comet, which it can't be."

"Why not?"

"Because of my new figures on its approach."

"Approach?" Broadsword asked.

"Oh yes, it's definitely headed this way. It should approach within five hundred thousand miles of earth if I'm right."

"Christ," Broadsword exclaimed. "That's within easy shuttle distance. I could take you that far right now."

"I know," Haskins said. "Whatever this thing is, we'll be able to get a close-up look at it."

"What's the speed now?"

"If you recall, in the first twenty-four hours I measured it, it traveled twenty million miles at a velocity of around eight hundred thousand miles per hour."

"I remember."

"In the past day, it's moved seventeen million, seven hundred and sixty thousand miles..."

"Wait a minute," Broadsword interrupted.

"...for an average speed of seven hundred forty thousand miles per hour," Haskins concluded.

"It's slowing down!"

"Quite so."

"That's impossible," Broadsword said. "It's heading toward the sun. If anything, the sun's gravity should be speeding it up."

"Exactly," Haskins said.

"Then what the hell...?"

"Is it? I still don't know."

"Could Jupiter's gravity be slowing it down?" Broadsword asked.

"I don't think so. It didn't appear to come close enough. However, I can check that back on Earth."

"There has to be something wrong with the computer," Broadsword said.

Haskins shook his head.

"Then Jupiter's slowing it down. There's no other explanation."

Haskins thought in silence, then nodded. "I suppose not," he said.

Broadsword pushed himself over to the travel tube. "I'll fire up the engines," he said.

"Can you fly me to Earth?" Haskins asked.

"Of course."

"Now?"

"Flying to Earth is a lot simpler than it used to be," Broadsword laughed, "but not that simple. I'm making the next Earth flight the day after tomorrow. If you want to go before then, you'll have to ask Edwards."

"I'll do that," Haskins said.

"I hope you have more luck with him than I do," Broadsword said.

"If he approves, are you free?"

Broadsword consulted his watch. "Right now I'm making another jog to the Moon."

"But you went there this morning."

"I'm going back."

"More miners to transport?" Haskins asked.

"No. This trip is personal. I'm flying with a friend who wants to show me a mining claim he's staked out. I'll be back in a few hours, after which I have a tennis date. Tomorrow, though, I can take you to Earth...if Edwards approves."

"I can't ask for more than that," Haskins said,

and started to bundle up his equipment.

Eichstadt Crater was a new formation toward the eastern limb of the near face of the Moon. It sat astride the Cordillera Mountains and formed a triangle with craters Darwin and Byrgius. Broadsword sat in the copilot's seat as Baxter brought the *Columbia* in over the Southeast Quadrant Navigation Beacon, erected atop the Kelvin Promontory on the edge of Mare Humorum once Moon flights became routine in the late 1980s. Then he cruised in low over Prosper Henry and Lamark, banking to starboard to land on the narrow strip his Moon skids had carved out on the lunar surface. Fine gray dust flew around the old spacecraft, and Broadsword held on for dear life.

"Are you sure this thing is safe?" he asked.

"Watch your tongue, boy. I might get the idea to leave you here."

"I might not get off this rock anyway. Are you sure your vertical thrusters work?"

"If they don't, neither of us is leavin'. Stop worrin' and put on your suit."

The *Columbia* still had the old series 100 shuttle suits, designed to fit most bodies apt to need them. They were bulky, weighed more than Broadsword himself and were hung from racks in the air-lock module. As Broadsword fumbled into one of them, Baxter shut down the *Columbia*'s engines and joined him.

"I should have had the sense to bring my FlexSuit," Broadsword said.

"You complain more than anyone I ever heard, boy. These old suits are plenty good for me. I come here to work, not play tennis."

"I should also have brought my racket. I could have put one in orbit."

They had finished suiting up, and Baxter depressurized the air lock. "When you gonna get serious about your life?" he asked.

"Not you too," Broadsword groaned. "I've been getting the same line from Leslie."

"She wants a secure future," Baxter said. "These young girls now aren't like the ones I knew when I was your age."

"Can you really remember that far back?"

"I'll remember that wisecrack. No, girls then would fuck a guy soon as look at him. Now, they all got glue between their knees. I thought I'd never live to see the day when a girl just outta her teens would want to inspect a guy's pension plan before goin' to bed with him."

"Life marches on," Broadsword said idly as the hatch swung open.

The surface was smooth, with only a few small impact craters marring the ground between the landing strip and the crater wall. Broadsword and Baxter hopped down and walked slowly across the few hundred yards of Moon dust, which swirled about their feet, clinging to everything.

"If your girl wants security, you ought to quit that chicken outfit you work for and partner up with me," Baxter said.

"Things are tough enough the way they are."

"I ain't kiddin', boy. In this ground here there's enough aluminum, titanium, iron and oxygen to make you and me rich men."

"Sure," Broadsword said.

"I mean it. I got samples of anorthosite, plagioclase and ilmenite—lots of ilmenite."

49

"All low grade ore," Broadsword said.

"So what? There's plenty of it."

"Suppose for a second I go along with this idiot scheme. We'd need a mining crew, equipment, housing, a better landing strip... my God, Curtiss, you're talking about millions."

"Financing can be arranged. A year ago when Von Rico went public with his mining operation proposal at La Pérouse, he was trading over-the-counter at ten bucks a share. As of yesterday, he was on the Big Board at fifty-two bucks a share. What do you say to that?"

"Von Rico was rich when he started."

"No he wasn't," Baxter said emphatically. "That's a lie the Moon Commission has been circulating 'cause they don't want to encourage private operations. I know how much money Von Rico had, and I got nearly as much. Between the two of us, we can swing it."

"I don't have any money to speak of," Broadsword maintained.

"You join up with me, after two Belt missions we'll have enough."

"Is this your idea of a secure future?"

"Sure it is." Baxter led Broadsword to a steep slope right at the bottom of the northwest crater wall. He knelt and, taking a small pick from his tool belt, chipped away at the rock face until a chunk came off.

"You see this?" Baxter asked, holding it up and getting to his feet. "You know what it is?"

"I see it, but I don't know what it is."

"Ilmenite, a good source of both titanium and iron."

"If you say so," Broadsword shrugged.

"I say so, and you're gonna say so once you hook up with me."

"You don't need me," Broadsword said. "You can fly two more Belt missions and get enough money yourself."

"Let's just say that I'd kinda like the company."

Broadsword looked up from the magnificent desolation of the Moon and up at the bright ring of H5 gleaming in the distance and, beyond it, to Earth. "I'll think about it," he said.

SIX

The bright blue-and-white marble of Earth grew larger until it took up the entire window of the *Ark Royal*. The lower Hemisphere Viewscreen, a large, circular monitor placed on the console between the pilot and copilot stations, showed the swirling white clouds of a large low pressure system over the central Pacific. In the two passenger seats directly behind Broadsword and Chambers, Leslie and Haskins watched the Earth approach with casual curiosity. What for most persons would be thrilling had become for Leslie a matter of routine; Haskins was too caught up in thoughts of his mysterious object to think of much else.

"Time?" Broadsword asked.

"Two forty-four, seventeen," Margot replied.

"Kick in Granny."

Margot nodded, touched a button on her panel and switched on the Galactic Ranging And Navigation device, developed ten years before to facilitate Earth-Moon navigation, help keep track of extrasolar system probes and coordinate things with observational astronomers. It worked through the NaviComputer, and there was no piece of space around the Earth or Moon it couldn't find.

"Granny's on," Margot said.

"What's all this about?" Haskins asked.

"We're checking to see if Granny can find her way around the microwave beam coming in from Solar Collector One," Broadsword replied.

"I thought the beam wasn't due to be turned on for another week."

"They're switching it on at one-twentieth power just for this occasion. There's no danger to the *Ark Royal* from flying through the beam, even when it's at full power. But there could be residual effects on people from the microwaves, so all aircraft will have to avoid the area. It's only ten miles wide at an atmospheric level, so there won't be too much trouble getting around the thing."

"Why are we testing Granny now?" Haskins asked, a bit impatiently.

"The price you have to pay for being flown to Earth a day early," Broadsword replied.

"Oh," Haskins said, chastised.

"This won't take us long, Dr. Haskins," Margot said. "We're coming up on the beam now."

Broadsword switched the controls to automatic and watched in silence as the NaviComputer, using the Granny navigation beams sent up from Earth stations, swerved the *Ark Royal* around the invisible microwave beam and then returned it to course.

"Test's over," Broadsword said, picking up the microphone.

"H5 Control, this is *Ark Royal.*"

"Go ahead, *Ark Royal,*" a man's voice replied.

"So that's what I sound like," Leslie said.

"More or less," Broadsword said. "H5 Control, Granny navigated perfectly around the beam and returned to previous course. Test is over."

"Acknowledged, *Ark Royal,* and thank you. Handing you over to Kennedy Control."

Broadsword checked the instruments and switched the radio to the frequency for Kennedy Space Center in Florida. "Kennedy Control, this is *Ark Royal.* Do you copy our position?"

"Affirmative, *Ark Royal,* we have you on Autoland track, cleared for landing runway 33, MSBLS and NaviLanding, you can make your deorbit burn."

"One seventy-five miles altitude," Margot reported, as Broadsword opened the forward thruster cove and fired the retro-engine.

The forward-pointing rocket made the craft shudder almost as much as the MBEs. Broadsword preferred the retros to the old series 100 deorbit system, which necessitated turning the craft around and firing the main engines to slow her down, and which would have made a reasonable approach to H5 nearly impossible. When the deorbit burn was over, Broadsword closed the cover, leaned back in his seat and yawned.

"We'll land in an hour," he said. "Wake me when it's over."

"What did you say?" Haskins exclaimed.

Margot laughed. "Broadsword doesn't like the automatic landing system," she said. "It bores him."

"I might as well be driving the Staten Island Ferry," he grumbled, and Leslie leaned forward to pat him consolingly on the head.

The *Ark Royal* continued down into the atmosphere. As the EpiSkin tiles burned off, the spacecraft seemed to glow. Sparks and shards of material flew by the windows, and the roar was deafening. Even Broadsword couldn't fail to be awed by it. The display went on for the better part of an hour, until at last Margot poked Broadsword on the shoulder.

"Thirty-four miles high, twelve minutes to touchdown. We're 550 miles downrange."

"Terrific," Broadsword said, looking out the window. He drummed his fingers on the console while Margot took over communications with Kennedy.

"Eighty-three thousand feet," she announced, "seventeen hundred miles an hour, five minutes thirty to touchdown. We're over Florida."

"Drop me off at Disney World," Broadsword said.

He watched the scenery as it appeared in the Lower Hemisphere Viewscreen, which showed a 180-degree picture of everything beneath the ship.

"Thirteen thousand three hundred, 424 miles an hour, seven point five miles downrange and eighty-six seconds to touchdown. We're in autoland interface."

Broadsword put his hand on the stick, and felt it as the NaviComputer moved it to bring the *Ark Royal* to an easy landing. "You don't mind if I play pilot and make believe I'm flying, do you?" he asked.

"Not me, boss," Margot replied.

"Twenty-two degrees glidescope, 358 miles an hour, two miles and thirty-two seconds to runway."

A short distance ahead, the long concrete strip that was Kennedy's runway 33 loomed before them.

"Flaring to one point five degrees, three-oh-eight miles an hour, one three five feet in the air and seventeen seconds to touchdown."

"Okay," Broadsword said, his interest picking up, "wheels down, fourteen seconds."

"Ninety feet altitude," Margot replied. "Two sixty-eight miles an hour...we're over the runway...two fifteen miles an hour."

The landscape was a blur in the window. After the expanse of space, to see buildings, trees and ground going by so near and so fast was dizzying. "Touchdown," Broadsword said, and felt relieved.

"You really hate things like autopilots, don't you?" Leslie asked as they walked, arm in arm, through the sand.

"Yeah," Broadsword replied.

"But...isn't it *easier* to let the computer dock the ship at H5...and land it at Kennedy?"

"Sure, if you happen to like things the easy way."

"Nathaniel..."

"Oh, I guess I'm asking too much. After all, landing, takeoff and docking take up around two percent of a flight. The rest of the time, I manage to get some real flying done. Even if it *does* piss Edwards off."

They left the quiet sanctuary of the Merritt Island Wildlife Refuge, adjacent to KSC at Cape Canaveral, and walked down the road to the spaceport. They'd been on Earth two days while the *Ark Royal* was being outfitted for its return to space and given a new cargo. Takeoff would be that afternoon, and Broadsword was due back at Kennedy Control for a flight briefing. Their two days had been wonderful. They walked, picnicked in the woods, swam and rented a catamaran for a day's sail along the coast. They took down the sail and let the boat drift in the idle afternoon breeze, stretched out on the deck and sunned themselves.

The road was narrow but well traveled, with electric trams carrying spaceport workers to and from the wildlife refuge whenever they'd earned a respite from computers and countdowns. NASA had finally learned that not everything in a man's world could be aluminum and vinyl. The new-found wisdom carried over even to the design of H5; the colony had to be more than just a space station. It needed trees and grass, sunrise and sunset, and a way to pretend you really weren't in a glass and metal donut hurtling through space. Lack of that insight had spelled the doom of habitats One through Four. No one had wanted to stay in them for long.

Broadsword flagged down a tram and helped Leslie into one of the open seats in the back. With a half-dozen others, they rode out of the forest and into KSC. The *Ark Royal* stood on pad 39A, re-fueled and with a new cargo, while technicians pored over it.

"Baxter is really pushing me to work with him," Broadsword said.

"He's still on that? I thought he'd give up the idea once he sobered up."

"So did I. It seems to be important to him. He

showed me his mining claim and everything. Seems to think we can make a fortune together, like Von Rico did."

"The Moon Commission frowns on private enterprise," Leslie said.

"A third of the Commission members are Russians and another third are guys from the European Space Community. You know how they like to have government run everything. It's easier to get away with lack of imagination in a bureaucracy."

"Then you *are* thinking of taking Baxter up on his offer?" she asked cautiously.

Broadsword turned to face her, and held her hands.

"Leslie ... I can't go on forever being a ferry captain."

"Nathaniel ..."

"Look at the *Ark Royal*," he said. "She's beautiful, but she has more ties to Earth than a boulder. I'd like to ... Oh, I don't know."

He turned away, leaned back in the seat and closed his eyes. Leslie squeezed his arm affectionately.

"There's the Mars Colony mission coming up in a few months ... and a Saturn mission next year. You could sign up for them. With your ability ..."

"There are dozens of guys who fly as well as I do."

"Nonsense," she replied firmly.

"And all of them have a knowledge of planetary astronomy, which you'd need in order to fly one of those missions. All I can do is fly."

"Nathaniel," she said pleadingly, "you're flying now."

"Sure, I coast back and forth from the Earth to H5 to the Moon. Every so often I go chasing an asteroid, for which I get slapped down by Edwards."

Leslie shook her head sadly and let go of his arm.

The tram came to a halt in front of the Spaceport Center, an office and control building slightly taller than the Tower in H5. Leslie remained silent as Broadsword led her to the tenth floor astronaut briefing room.

The room was of the conference variety typical to small corporations. The walls were covered with imitation wood paneling, and plexiglass frames held color photographs of shuttle launches. On a Formica conference table sat a white plastic replica of the *Columbia* as it looked when first fired into orbit fifteen years earlier.

Nathaniel and Leslie sat at the middle of the table, alongside astronomer Haskins and across from Admiral William A. Jenson, last commander of the battleship-carrier *H.M.S. Lion* and the European Space Agency's expert in fleet operations. In semi-retirement, he ran shuttle operations at Kennedy Space Center and dreamed of the old days of military adventure. Broadsword liked Jenson; the man had imagination.

The admiral lit a cigar and tapped a finger on the papers in front of him. "Damned paperwork will be the death of me," he grumbled. "How are you, Broadsword? Dixon? Where'd you go this afternoon?"

"Black Cove," Broadsword said.

"Yes, a bit swampy this time of year, isn't it?"

"Very, but I got a picture of a brown pelican.

There aren't too many of them left."

"More than you think, and increasing every year, thank God. I get to the refuge as often as I can. Helps me forget the paperwork."

Broadsword nodded knowingly.

"Anyway, Broadsword, there's not too much to tell you. It's a fairly routine flight. I gave the specifics to your copilot, who's over supervising the preflight checks now. Haskins is going back up, and with him two of his colleagues. There will also be two men who will work to get Solar Collector One ready to be turned on at full power next week."

Broadsword nodded again.

"In that regard, we've made a little modification in the *Ark Royal*," Jenson went on. "We've installed microwave shields in the paneling around the crew's compartment. That means you'll be able to fly through the beam from SC1, even when it's at full strength. It will be standard to have Granny navigate around the beam anyway, but we're putting the shields in all ten craft just in case."

"I see."

"As for Doctor Haskins, we're of the opinion he may be onto something with this mysterious object of his. Now, we don't know what it is either, but it won't do any harm to try to find out. I'd like you to stay at his disposal in case he needs to use the Cassegrain."

"Sure thing," Broadsword replied. "What cargo am I carrying?"

Admiral Jenson handed him a sheaf of papers, which Broadsword read with growing disbelief.

"I didn't know there was this much food and

booze in the world," he said.

Jenson laughed. "For the opening day ceremonies on H5. We'll be sending up a few hundred dignitaries and potential colonists. NASA has decided to give them a good time."

Broadsword was appalled. "This is outrageous," he said, standing and folding the papers into a pocket.

"It's a goddam waste of the cargo bay, if you ask me," Jenson agreed, standing and shaking Broadsword's hand. "But I don't make the rules. That was a nice shot you made on that asteroid the other day, by the way."

"You tracked it?"

"Sure. I couldn't have got that rock better myself. If you ever get the notion your talent's being wasted here, I can get you into a good fighter squadron."

Broadsword laughed, and didn't notice the pained expression on Leslie's face.

SEVEN

Leslie had been crying for an hour. Her eyes were red and swollen, and her breath came in great, despairing gulps. They were in the garden between their apartment buildings, alone beneath a sapling maple. "It just isn't fair," she cried.

Broadsword touched her shoulder, but she pulled away.

"You can't do this to yourself," she went on. "You can't do it to *me!*"

Broadsword was exasperated. He'd expected a hard time of it, but not that hard a time. Most of all, he found her attitude impossible to understand. They'd been good friends for a year, and recently dated a handful of times, not counting the weekend on the Cape. Broadsword couldn't imagine how she could feel so strongly about him, and in fact consider him a vital part of her future, without having gone to bed with him. Perhaps he could have secured her favor by signing a long-term, no-escape contract with NASA and shown her his pension plan. But Broadsword wasn't ready to buy her approval and was growing a little angry.

"I'm not doing anything to *you*," he said. "I may be taking a chance with *my* future, but I even doubt that. I'm asking for a leave of absence, not quitting."

"It amounts to the same thing. You know Mr. Edwards will take the chance to be rid of you once and for all."

"Like I told you, he doesn't have the votes in Council. I'll be able to come back if it doesn't work out with Curtiss."

"Even if that's true," she continued, "I won't *see* you. You'll be making two trips to the Asteroid Belt...be gone for months."

"I'll come back at the end, and then you'll see enough of me to make you sick."

Impulsively, Leslie pulled his head down to hers and kissed him.

"Don't you love me?" she asked.

Broadsword was startled; the word had never passed between them before.

"Yes," he said, "of course."

"And I love you. I want us to have a future."

"We will. If it doesn't work out with Baxter and me, I'll go right back to playing ferry captain. Hauling food and booze from Earth to H5. Christ!"

Leslie backed away from him, her own anger building.

"If you loved me as you say, you'd give me a future," she cried.

Broadsword's temper finally snapped. "If *you* loved *me*, you'd give me something, too." Then, realizing he'd gone too far, added quickly, "A little bit of trust."

64

It was too late. Breaking into sobs again, Leslie wheeled and ran down the path toward her flat. Broadsword watched her until she was out of sight, then kicked viciously at a piece of dirt.

He strode to the lobby of the Tower and rode the elevator to the Council offices on the fortieth floor. Edwards was at his desk, behind the usual stack of papers. In contrast to Admiral Jenson, Edwards seemed to enjoy paperwork.

"You wanted to see me, Broadsword?" he asked with some curiosity. Broadsword had never before asked to see *him*.

"I'd like a leave of absence."

Edwards' eyebrows arched upwards. "May I ask why?"

"I plan to go into business with Curtiss Baxter," Broadsword replied.

"I see. So we're going to have *two* independent prospectors, is that it?"

"Yes, sir."

"Well, I won't pretend I'd miss you," Edwards said.

"Thank you for that. I can use some clarity in my life."

"Okay, Broadsword, you can have your leave of absence. How long would you like it for? Six months, a year, or open-ended?"

"A year. But I'd like the chance to come back if it doesn't work out with Baxter."

"No doubt you would."

"We *are* being honest," Broadsword replied.

"It's fine with me," Edwards said. "Maybe in a year from now you'll have settled down a bit and will have learned the value of working for a major enterprise like this."

"Maybe," Broadsword allowed.

"On the other hand, maybe you'll have become a wealthy man. Who knows?" He consulted his desk calendar, and made a notation on a page. "You can start your leave of absence in a month . . . no, five weeks."

"I was hoping to start it right away," Broadsword said, a bit puzzled.

"Out of the question. As much as I'd like to be rid of you, the next month will be a hectic one, and I need all the pilots I can get. There's the switch-on of Solar Collector One next week . . . and the grand opening celebration of H5 in thirty days."

"And you need me to haul home the empties," Broadsword said.

"Among other things, yes. There is also the matter of Dr. Haskins."

"What about him?"

Edwards tossed his hands up in bewilderment. "It seems," he said, "that the object he spotted is of much greater interest than it looked as recently as this morning. In the two days you were down on Earth, it decelerated to five hundred thousand miles per hour and now seems to be holding at that speed. It's heading in this direction and is calculated to pass by Earth in about three weeks from now."

"Does he know what the hell it is yet?" Broadsword asked.

"There is some talk," Edwards said with great reluctance, "and *just* talk, about the possibility of its being a spacecraft."

"What?" Broadsword exclaimed. "That's a crock if ever I heard one."

"I agree. For one thing, it appears to be oddly shaped and about two miles in one dimension. Possibly larger in another dimension."

"Too big, too fast and too far from any conceivable home."

"We're in complete agreement. However, NASA is very excited about it and has given Haskins carte blanche. And the doctor wants you to stay on call to fly him, his instruments and his colleagues around until they determine what it is that's headed our way."

"My God."

"I'll make a deal with you, Broadsword... you stay on another five weeks, and you can have your leave of absence—for as long as you want—with the guarantee of your old job back whenever you want it. If you insist on leaving right away, you can just quit and get any notion out of your head of ever working for NASA again."

"This sounds like the kind of deal they offered Napoleon after Waterloo," Broadsword said, agreeing to it just the same.

Baxter and Chambers were already half-tanked by the time Broadsword joined them. The Sky Inn was filled then, mostly with miners on their way home from three-month tours of duty at the Copernicus colony on the Moon. An antique jukebox blared an old jazz tune, and a lively poker game in one corner drew a large crowd of spectators. Broadsword wore a slightly sheepish look as he joined his friends at the bar.

"How'd it go, boy?" Baxter asked, handing Broadsword a bottle of Coke.

"He said 'okay.'"

"Great! When do we start?"

"Not for five weeks," Broadsword admitted.

"How come so long? I'd like to take off for the Belt in a day or so."

"We made a deal. I can always get my job back as long as I stick around long enough to handle the increased traffic between now and opening day."

Baxter shrugged. "If that's how it's got to be," he said. "I can do some work on my claim, maybe pull a bargeload or two out of there."

"How did Leslie take the news?" Margot asked.

"I haven't seen her since I talked to Edwards. She's pretty upset, though. And I lost my head and said a few things I shouldn't have this afternoon."

"She'll get over it as soon as she sees the money in your wallet from our operations," Baxter said, finishing his beer and ordering another round.

"I don't know."

"Trust me, boy. I know all there is to know about women."

"You know enough to get by," Margot said.

"Would you listen to her?" Baxter chided. "She'll be singin' a different tune once you and me take off for parts unknown, leavin' her stuck behind without a captain. She'll have to get off her ass and get her captain's license at last."

"Not me, old man," Margot said. "I'm coming with you two."

"What?" Baxter exclaimed.

"That's right. I'm gonna fly the *Columbia* while you two fucks float around in space, chipping away at rocks."

"Two partners is enough," Baxter said. "Ain't that right, boy?"

"Keep me out of this," Broadsword replied with a laugh. "I have woman problems of my own."

"I'm coming no matter what you say," Margot insisted. "I've grown fond of Geronimo here, and I don't mean to let him get away so easily."

"I've got to go," Broadsword said, finishing his drink. "I'm due to spend tomorrow flying Haskins around."

"Not again!" Margot exclaimed. "I thought you were done with him."

"So did I. But Haskins seems to have convinced NASA that his mysterious object is a U.F.O. coming here to say hello to us."

"Wonderful," Baxter mumbled, "another goddam looney bin, as if we don't have enough already."

"The thing's settled down to cruising speed now," Broadsword went on, "a modest half-million miles an hour, and should be about halfway between Jupiter and Mars."

"In the Belt!" Baxter said, with mock anger. "The fuckin' thing's after our rocks!"

Broadsword slapped his friend on the back and his empty bottle down on the bar. "I'm going home," he said.

"No you're not," Baxter said. "You're staying and watching us get drunk." He ordered another Coke and handed it to Broadsword.

"I have to work tomorrow."

"When? Right after breakfast?"

"Eleven."

"Then you'll stay and drink with your friends," Baxter said. "We have something to celebrate this evening."

Broadsword fumbled open the door to his flat shortly after one in the morning. He'd spent the whole evening with Baxter and Chambers, playing pinball and singing along with the jukebox, and joining an expedition to the hub to play Zero Gravity Soccer. He locked the door behind him and walked to the bath, shedding clothes all the way. He went straight into the shower and spent a long time under the refreshing stream of water before toweling off and walking into the bedroom stark naked, drying his hair.

There was the sound of a woman's voice clearing her throat. Startled, Broadsword saw Leslie sitting up in his bed, wearing one of his Western shirts, the sheet pulled up to her waist. He quickly moved the towel from his head to his loins.

"Oh," he said, a bit embarrassed, "hi."

"You've been out all night," she said with a smile.

"Yeah, I guess I have."

"I don't blame you. I behaved awfully today."

"I'm not too proud of the way I carried on, either," Broadsword replied, sitting on the side of the bed.

Leslie reached out and touched his shining black hair. "You're wet," she said.

"I just took a shower."

"Come here."

She pulled him to her, and held his head to her breast. "I talked to Mr. Edwards after you saw him," she said. "He told me about your agreement."

"Yeah, I'm gonna be pretty safe. If Curtiss and I can't hack it on our own, I can come running back to NASA with my tail between my legs."

Leslie stroked his hair. "I guess I was afraid you'd go running off into space and I'd never see you again."

"There's no chance of that."

"Let me dry your hair. You're getting me all wet."

Broadsword sat up. "I'll get another towel."

"This one will do," Leslie said, quickly snatching it from around his waist. She pulled his head back to her and rubbed his hair dry. Then she tossed the towel across the room.

"What are you doing?" he asked, turning toward her.

"Isn't it obvious?" she asked.

"Yeah, but..."

"Shut up."

Leslie unbuttoned the shirt and tossed it after the towel. Her breasts were perfectly formed, with brilliant, plum-colored nipples. She pulled his head down to them.

Broadsword had wanted her all along, but had stayed at least fairly respectful of her prerogative. As one of the few women in space, surrounded by men, the pressure on her was terrific and the response predictable. Women in space were protective of their reputations. They tended not to be as free as they would have liked. Leslie was, at last, being free, and he loved it.

His hands roamed her small body, compact but full of wonder. The thought of her going so far to seduce him was exciting. She held him in her hands, and he kissed her breasts, his hands pushing open her thighs, fingers slipping inside her.

"I've wanted you so long," she whispered. "I just had to know how you felt." And she pulled him into her.

EIGHT

Broadsword and Haskins rode the elevator to the rim, their arms full of tape cassettes, computer printouts and film cannisters. The day's session had been a long one, involving both optical and radio astronomy observations, and Broadsword had flown it tired half to death from the night before. He was eager to get back to his apartment, where Leslie was cooking a brace of lobsters which the captain of the *Lexington*, with his customarily astounding dexterity, had managed to smuggle up from Earth.

"Where do you want all this stuff?" Broadsword asked.

"I've been given an office on the eighth floor of the Tower. Do you mind helping me?"

"No. I've got time. But I'd like to take the tram. I don't think I could make it through the park in my condition."

"Have a busy night?" Haskins laughed.

"Busier than you could imagine."

The elevator deposited them by the tram station, and they got right into a car. A few minutes later, Haskins and Broadsword were in a large office complex, made up of one large room partitioned off into ribbed glass cubicles.

Haskins put the data on an otherwise vacant receptionist's desk in the front of the office.

"Thank you," he said.

"Don't mention it. Tomorrow, same time?"

"That will be fine," Haskins replied.

Broadsword went to the door, then paused and turned back toward the astronomer. "Are you really serious about the U.F.O. business?" he asked.

"I'd like not to be. Talking about U.F.O.'s is the quickest way to kill a career I know of. But there's simply no other explanation."

"Computer malfunction?" Broadsword asked, walking toward Haskins.

"I'm afraid not."

"A gremlin in the telescope optics?"

Haskins shook his head.

"How about a large asteroid...perhaps a previously unnoticed moon of Jupiter...which has spun out of orbit and which was slowed down as it moved out of Jupiter's gravity."

"That is the most plausible explanation other than a U.F.O.," Haskins said. "Equally plausible is a piece of interstellar garbage that wandered into our systems at an incredible speed and then was slowed down by Jupiter."

"Well?" Broadsword asked.

"It didn't come close enough to Jupiter to be that affected. Furthermore, how do you explain the extraordinary deceleration? A natural object simply wouldn't slow down as rapidly as it did, then assume a static velocity of five hundred thousand miles per hour. It would slow down at a slow but steady rate. No, I'm afraid the only explanation that fits the facts is an interstellar spacecraft."

Broadsword sat on the edge of the receptionist's desk and folded his arms. "I don't know much about astronomy," he said. "I've told you that. However, I do know about flying and space travel, and I've read some about extraterrestrial intelligence."

"Go on," Haskins said.

"There has never been the slightest bit of evidence for the existence of any civilization anywhere in the universe other than right here."

"Some recent opinion has it that Earth may, in fact, be unique," Haskins agreed. "I've read the same things you have."

"All the arguments for other civilizations are pure conjecture. That planet formation is a frequent result of star formation. That life is a frequent result of planet formation. And that life, once established on a stable planet, will inevitably grow to become intelligent."

"And given the number of stars in the universe..."

"There must be civilizations elsewhere. About once every fourteen light years, if I recall."

"I've heard as often as once every six light years," Haskins said.

"To fly fourteen light years, even at eight hundred thousand miles an hour," Broadsword said, "would take hundreds of years."

"Ah," Haskins said triumphantly, "but if they were going *faster* than that. Flying at nearly the speed of light, it could be done in...let me see...around a week. That's from the point of view of the travelers and taking relativity into account."

"Nothing can reach the speed of light," Broadsword said. "Other than light."

"I said *nearly* the speed of light. Anyway, it is all conjecture. Let's keep watching that thing and find out what it is. Very likely it'll turn out to be what we said—an errant piece of interstellar junk which happened to wander our way and is now going through the Asteroid Belt."

"Wait a second," Broadsword said excitedly. "When it slowed to half-a-million miles an hour, where was it? In the Belt?"

"Unh...yes. Why?"

"It could have collided with an asteroid. That would slow it rather abruptly, maybe even to a constant speed."

"Of course!" Haskins said excitedly. "It could have hit an asteroid! At the speed it was traveling, it could have pulverized the asteroid without being deflected into another course! But it would have been slowed dramatically! Damn it, why didn't I think to ask a pilot for his opinion before? That's just the sort of thing a pilot would think of but an astronomer wouldn't."

Flushed with pride, Broadsword pushed away from the desk and went one more time to the door.

"You may just have saved my career, Captain," Haskins said.

"I hate to admit it, but I'm getting kind of interested in this matter," Broadsword said. "How'd you like it if I arrange a triangulation on it for you?"

"We're triangulating now. I'm coordinating with Palomar."

"I mean a *real* triangulation. Tomorrow, the *Hood* is flying a group of Russians over to the Solar Collector Two construction site. That's 22,-300 miles to the far side of Earth from us once every day. We could load up the *Hood*'s cargo bay with another Cassegrain unit and have one of your guys run it."

"Excellent idea. That would give us a triangulation base of nearly a quarter-million miles. Thank you, Captain."

"I'll get right on it," Broadsword said as he slipped out the door.

Lying in bed later that night, with Leslie's hair spread across his shoulder, Broadsword felt at ease for the first time in quite a while. He was in love. He was on the brink of a great adventure. In five weeks he'd be on his way to the Asteroid Belt with Baxter and, God knows, even Margot. They'd hunt minerals, explore a bit, laugh a lot and maybe get rich. Maybe he'd ask Leslie to marry him after things settled down. They'd have children—the first born away from Earth. It would all be wonderful. To Broadsword, nothing could be better.

Every moment, the great object which had come so far through the blackness of interstellar space drew closer. With Broadsword's help, Haskins and his colleagues on Earth and H5 watched it. The trajectory had been plotted, and it turned out to be an extraordinary one, scarcely a trajectory at all. It was as if the object were flying straight toward Earth, unaffected by the sun's gravity. As it neared, the dimensions were refined. It was two miles in width, a mile high and at least ten miles long. With that information, Haskins' fears for his career disappeared. No ship could be that big. The propulsion problems alone would be momentous. The mysterious object was tentatively classified as a large asteroid with an extremely eccentric orbit. When it was, it dropped out of the headlines on Earth. The big space stories became the successful switch-on of Solar Collector One, and its transmission to the receiving station in Nebraska of enough power to light a quarter of the nation. The start of construction on Solar Collector Two in a fixed orbit over the Soviet Union attracted quite a lot of interest in the Old World. As Broadsword began his final two weeks in the service of NASA, everyone was talking about the upcoming grand opening of H5. Haskins' Object—for that is what it had come to be called—was all but forgotten.

Even Broadsword had lost interest in the matter. His daily flights in the service of astronomy were once again the drudge they seemed at the start. So when he left H5 on a particularly innocuous Wednesday, Broadsword was pleased when Margot decided to come with him. For one thing, it saved him from feeling obliged to resurrect the sneezing experiments.

They ferried Haskins out to the usual spot a short distance from H5 where his Cassegrain would be unaffected by the lights of the space station, and left him to his own devices. They remained in the pilots' compartment, watching a rebeamed broadcast of an old John Wayne movie on one of the utility screens. After watching the actor lead a fighter squadron into victorious battle against the Japanese in World War II, Margot abruptly shut off the monitor.

"What's the matter?" he asked.

"Who said something's the matter?" she replied, a bit unconvincingly.

"You wouldn't be out here with me when you could be back at H5 goofing off with Curtiss."

"He's busy today. He's negotiating for fuel and provisions for the first Belt trip you two are going to make."

"What takes so long about that?" Broadsword asked.

"They want two forty-seven a unit for the fuel. He's trying to get them to come down a bit."

"It still doesn't take all day. Why don't you tell me what the problem is?"

"You're getting annoyingly perceptive for a child," Margot said, now visibly nervous. "God . . . I wish I had a smoke."

"Not in here, kid. You'd light up alarms all over the place."

She sighed. "It's Curtiss. I . . . Christ, I never thought I'd be telling my troubles to a 24-year-old."

"Get on with it," Broadsword snapped.

"I . . . want to join you two. I want to quit NASA and go along. Part of it's wanting to be with Curtiss. I guess I'm getting fond of the old fart. Another part of it's not wanting to miss the fun. But Jesus, I . . ."

"You're scared."

"I am," she admitted. "I haven't got the nerve. Dammit, I'm the only woman pilot in the shuttle service. There's only room for one, and if I leave

79

there's no way I'm coming back. That little bitch Jenny Dinkins will be up from Kennedy so fast it will make your head spin. Then what the hell will I do? There'll be no coming back for me."

"In case the great mining expeditions don't work out," Broadsword said.

"Exactly. I don't have the options you do."

"There's only one choice for you," he said. "You have to stay. Maybe even take the captain's test."

"Who will I fly with? Everyone else is one of those goddam golf pros NASA seems to have cornered the market on. I hate to say it in so many words, Broadsword, but I'm getting goddam fond of you, too. So much so I'm starting to get jealous of Leslie. Jesus, what am I saying?"

Broadsword laughed, leaned over, held her chin and forced a kiss on her. For a split second, she nearly became passionate. Then she yanked her head away and lapsed into mock anger.

"Watch your ass, Broadsword...I might take you up on it."

"Stay with NASA and take the captain's test," he said. "You'll get your own ship...maybe even the *Ark Royal*. On the other hand, if you screw it up and don't make captain, I'll probably be back and things will be the same as always."

Margot bobbed her head up and smiled in gratitude. "Nathaniel, I..."

She was interrupted by a shout which made it all the way in from the Cassegrain Observation Segment.

"Captain! Captain Broadsword!"

It was Haskins. "Science never sleeps," Broadsword said, and led the way to where the astronomer stood surrounded by instruments. Haskins peered at his main monitor, on which a large, white object flew in front of the starfield.

"There it is!" he exclaimed. "The first clear picture!"

Broadsword and Chambers made their way to the screen and joined Haskins in looking at it. The object was still far-off and quite indistinct.

"It looks like a big arrowhead," Broadsword said, fascinated.

"It's phenomenal," Haskins went on. "Ten miles long, and a mile deep . . . a bit more than two miles wide and . . . yes, you're right . . . shaped like an arrowhead."

"How far away is it now?" Margot asked.

"From us or from Earth?"

"Us."

"We're nearer to it than Earth," Haskins said. "Let's see." He punched a few buttons, and figures appeared on another monitor. "About one hundred thousand miles."

"In other words," Broadsword said, "it'll be on top of us in twelve minutes."

"No. That's the other thing. It's slowed down again. To less than twenty thousand miles an hour."

"What!"

"This time you have to be right. It has to be a computer malfunction," Haskins said quickly.

"It's almost as if it's slowing down to see what it's getting itself into," Margot said.

Broadsword felt his mind catch fire. "Are you finished here, Doctor?" he asked.

"Unh . . . yes."

"Then pack up the stuff and come up in the

front. We're gonna settle the question of what the hell that is right now."

Margot needed no prompting. "I'll fire her up," she said, and dived into the travel tube with a finesse that would have done Broadsword proud.

NINE

The *Ark Royal* shuddered as the three Multi-Burn Engines pushed it forward at slightly more than fifty-thousand miles per hour. Broadsword kept the throttles all the way forward until the craft reached maximum speed, then backed them off and let the ship coast. As silence once again returned to the cockpit, he picked up the microphone.

"*Ark Royal* to H5 Control."

"H5 Control," Leslie replied.

"We are flying course 2797.3 by 9936 to investigate Haskins' Object. ETA of return seven o'clock."

Leslie was silent for a time, then her voice came back.

"*Ark Royal*, is this an official flight?"

"Yes it is," Broadsword replied.

"Very well...but be careful, Nathaniel."

"I'll try," he replied, and put down the mike.

"Isn't love wonderful," Margot said.

"I see you're feeling better."

Haskins was in one of the passengers' seats and leaned forward to talk to Broadsword.

"How close will you come to it?" he asked.

"I'm not getting within fifty thousand miles of that thing," Broadsword replied. "I'll fly you by it, we'll shoot some pictures, then run like hell for home. I'm not taking any chances."

"But if it's only an asteroid..."

"Neither of us believes that anymore, Doctor," Broadsword said. "It's going into orbit around the Earth...it's slowed down...made course changes ...it flies straight on without tumbling, which is inconceivable for a random bit of space junk. It has to be a ship."

Haskins shook his head in disbelief. "If only I could use the Cassegrain."

"You can," Margot said. "I can run it from up here...pipe the pictures to one of the utility screens."

"There's no reason we can't run with the cargo bay doors open," Broadsword said. "And when coasting the ship is just as stable as when it's sitting still."

Margot climbed out of her seat and drifted to the aft of the cockpit, where the cargo handling instruments were located. She opened the doors and, within a few minutes, had tied the telescope controls into the utility panel at the copilot's station. Back in her seat, she punched buttons until one of the screens over the window flashed an image of the starfield.

"Do you have Granny coordinates for the object?" she asked.

Haskins fumbled through his papers for a time.

"Here's the last trajectory," he said, showing her a computer printout.

Margot punched the numbers into her computer. "Let's see . . . we've been moving for twelve minutes on an intersecting course. . . . Christ, this is going to take a minute! Okay . . . okay, I got it."

She fed the Granny numbers into the Navi-Computer and almost immediately a picture of Haskins' Object appeared on the utility screen. It was still small, but the shape was clear. The object was pure white, and looked very much like an elongated arrowhead. Margot fiddled with the computer to make the picture clearer.

"That'll have to do for the time being," she said. "But in half an hour we'll be pretty close to it and get some halfway decent shots."

"Start the camera," Broadsword said. "One frame every thirty seconds for now, one a second when we're close. I'm gonna bank at fifty thousand miles, turn up and to starboard, crossing her bow. Make sure you kick in the port cameras when we turn."

"Sure thing, boss."

"Did you say 'bow'?" Haskins asked.

"That's right, Doctor. And Margot . . . feed the pictures back to H5, would you?"

Margot gave her captain a concerned look. "You really think that's necessary?"

Haskins agreed. "After all," he added, "we *will* be going back." He looked at Broadsword and Chambers, then at the object. "Won't we?"

"I think so," Broadsword replied. "But I still have a bad feeling about that thing. Its arrival looks to be anything but coincidental, and plans for my future that I don't know about worry me."

Margot was on the radio. "H5, *Ark Royal* here, prepare to receive optical telemetry on Haskins' Object."

"Acknowledge, *Ark Royal*," Leslie replied.

"Telemetry's going through," Margot reported after a time.

"Nothing to do now but wait," Broadsword said, leaning back in his seat, his hands behind his head.

The wait was not to be long. The great white object grew steadily larger, both on the monitor and through the forward window, as the *Ark Royal* and it approached one another. The three persons in the shuttle watched the screen with a combination of curiosity and dread, like sailors frozen with awe by an approaching tornado.

Broadsword stared, rapt, as the image on the screen grew until some detail could be seen. A slice of darkness cut across the bow like a mouth. More likely it was a huge cockpit window, from which God-knows-what stared out at the tiny *Ark Royal*. The sides were like barbs; along them were dark spots, black and regularly shaped. The stern couldn't be seen, nor any more detail. Broadsword had no doubt what it was. Haskins, however, wavered. No doubt he would have preferred to have his name attached to a harmless chunk of rock.

"Look at the cratering," he exclaimed, more than a little desperately, "the pockmarks down the side! It must have been under heavy bombardment going through the Asteroid Belt!"

Broadsword wrapped his fingers around the throttles.

"That's no asteroid, Doctor, and those aren't pockmarks. They're gun ports."

He pushed the throttles all the way forward. The *Ark Royal*'s three engines roared into life, and the fragile craft shook like never before as Broadsword put her into a sweeping turn up and away.

TEN

H5 was in bedlam by the time the *Ark Royal* docked at bay 7 and its three occupants debarked. The entire Council as well as Curtiss Baxter and three of the half-dozen shuttle pilots on the station at the time met Broadsword at the docking bay, brimming over with questions and apprehension. Clutching his data cartridges and computer print-outs, Haskins followed Margot Chambers out of the *Ark Royal* and onto the dock.

Baxter elbowed his way to the front of the crowd and offered a comradely grin. "What happened, boy? You bite off more than you can chew out there?"

"That thing is no asteroid," Broadsword said. "It's a fucking ship."

"It does kinda look that way," Baxter said. "I watched the monitor with your little girl friend . . . happened to be passin' by Control when your telemetry came in. That's some kind of ship. What is it? Ten miles long?"

"At least."

Baxter whistled softly. "In that case, let's hope she's friendly."

"Friendly ships don't carry guns," Broadsword said.

"You're an infant. Everyone's armed in one way or another."

"*Not* with ten miles of gun ports."

There was a rustling amid the crowd, and Howard Edwards appeared. He looked frustrated and angry, as if one of the most momentous events in Earth history—contact with another civilization—meant only another thorn in his side. Broadsword felt the situation keenly. As one of the long time thorns in Edwards' side, he would have preferred that someone else bring the bad news.

"All right, Broadsword," Edwards snapped, "what's this all about?"

"I think you know," Broadsword replied.

"I saw your pictures. Now, what makes you so sure it's a ship, let alone a hostile one? You looked at a ten-mile-long object from a distance of fifty thousand miles."

"Through the 20-inch Cassegrain," Broadsword said quickly.

"Nonetheless..."

"If it's any help, Mr. Edwards," Haskins cut in, "I'm also convinced the object is a space vessel. Maybe I can settle the question by going right now to the observatory in the hub and trying the 100-inch telescope on it."

"All right, Doctor," Edwards breathed, "go ahead and do it. Pipe the pictures up to the fortieth floor briefing room. We'll wait for them there."

Haskins disappeared, taking his data with him.

"You needn't use a telescope at all," Broadsword said. "The goddam thing was right behind us all the way. It'll be on top of us in less than an hour. You'll be able to throw rocks at it, then."

Edwards' temper flared. "I've had enough of your lip, Captain. I'll see you and Commander Chambers in the briefing room right away." And he turned and stalked off.

Baxter tossed a mock punch at Broadsword. "Better learn how to duck, boy," he said. "A lot of shit's gonna be flyin' your way."

The fortieth floor briefing room was a sort of chapel, with a gigantic viewscreen in place of an altar, and rows of functional fiberglass seats replacing pews. A raised platform stood in front of the viewscreen, which was flanked by the flag of the United States and the banner of Habitat Five. There was even a long pointer such as might be used in classrooms. Indeed, the briefing room was a classroom, though to that point it had been used mainly to discuss lunar trajectories and shipping schedules. Being on the top floor of the Tower, the room fit snugly into the inner curve of the rim. Two walls and the ceiling were rounded and made of glass, allowing a clear view of the heavens once the curtains were pulled back.

Edwards was already there when Broadsword and Chambers arrived. Leslie Dixon had been pressed into service to run the viewscreen. She waved apprehensively to Broadsword, then got back to the job of bringing in the picture Haskins would send from the hub observatory.

Edwards paced up and down the small stage, trying to make sense out of this latest calamity.

Broadsword and Chambers took seats in the front row and watched him until he stopped and faced them.

"I have delayed telling NASA about this ...ship...of yours until there is more conclusive evidence," he said.

"I don't know how much more you need. The damn thing doesn't behave like a natural object."

"Neither did black holes until we figured out what they were. Really, Captain, you were the one who described the 'ship' theory as being a crock."

"That was before I saw it close up," Broadsword argued.

"From fifty thousand miles, you mean. And don't tell me about the Cassegrain. Miss Dixon, do you have the picture from the hub observatory yet?"

"Very soon, Mr. Edwards," Leslie replied, without turning to face him.

Edwards began pacing again and talking to himself, but quite out loud. "What if it's true? My God...and the opening of H5 coming up next week."

"I'd suggest you cancel the party," Broadsword chimed in. "Either that or make sure you invite our new friends."

Edwards spun on Broadsword in anger. "Captain, I ..."

But he was interrupted by Leslie, who had been on the phone to the hub.

"Mr. Edwards?" she said.

"Yes, *what?*" he spat.

"Dr. Haskins said he can't send us a picture."

"Why not? He's using the 100-inch, for God's sake!"

"The object is too clase. He said..." Leslie paused a second, and looked a bit embarrassed. "May I tell you his exact words, sir?"

"Yes, dammit, tell me!"

"Dr. Haskins said to look out the fucking window."

She pressed the button to pull back the drapes. As the fabric moved aside and the room darkened, they all looked up to see a mammoth battle cruiser, all angular and gleaming white, bristling with antennas and armaments. It looked like the biggest battleship of World War II, only glued keel-to-keel to a twin and enlarged a hundredfold. What seemed from a distance like an arrowhead was the largest warship imaginable, with fighting decks on top and bottom, and along each side a row of mammoth ports. What looked from a distance of fifty thousand miles like a window across the bow was a gigantic painted symbol, resembling a streak of lightning but meant, no doubt, to be the gaping maw of a shark.

Leslie gasped and backed away from the glass. Broadsword went to her. Margot stood in awe and Edwards was paralyzed in his tracks. The ship moved past H5 slowly, and with elegant menace, its ten-mile length seeming to take hours to pass. For a time, the warship blotted out the Moon, the sun and the stars; all that could be seen were turrets, antennas, decks and more guns than seemed possible to build.

As it passed, Broadsword left Leslie and walked, transfixed, to the window. He stared at the warship as it moved away, to take up an orbit around

Earth, its engines emitting a pale yellow glow. When it was gone, he turned and faced the others.

"A hundred years ago," he said, "American presidents had the custom of sending our biggest battleships past troublesome foreign countries by way of scaring the pants off them."

Broadsword paused, sucked in his breath, and finished his thought. "I'd say the same thing has just been done to us."

ELEVEN

There was no way to keep the electrifying news from Earth. In an instant, Man knew he was not unique, that Earth wasn't an aberration of the cosmos, but just one among many and by no means the most powerful. The gods of ancient Greece had returned, and who the hell would say that they might not resume hurling thunderbolts? Overnight, religions were rewritten, scientists speculated with remarkable élan and military chiefs of staff worried.

The great warship began to orbit the Earth a short distance beyond the Moon. Not a word came from it—no messages of any kind. For two days it orbited, frightening the daylights out of all who heard of it. World space interests were at that time controlled by the United Nations Space Commission, of which the principal members were the United States, the European Space Community and the Soviet Union. Following two panic sessions, it was decided to handle all negotiations with the visitors through H5. The colony had, after all, been of sufficient interest to the aliens to cause them to buzz it on their way into Earth orbit.

Broadsword found himself at the center of the dilemma. He had been the first Earthman to recognize a ship from another star system, and he insisted on remaining at the center of things. He'd wanted adventure, and for a time thought he could find it poking around the Asteroid Belt with Curtiss Baxter. But all thoughts of that enterprise vanished when the warship arrived. Instead, he spent time sitting in H5 Control with Leslie as she tried to contact the intruder.

Despite messages sent in various languages and in several binary codes which any life forms intelligent enough for space travel should be able to understand, there was no reply. For three days Leslie broadcast messages of peace and requests for face-to-face contact and was greeted only with silence. Finally, the attempt was abandoned. The Commission wanted a more direct approach. H5 was ordered to send a shuttle out to the warship with a peace mission aboard. They were to fly to within a mile of the ship, broadcasting peace messages continuously, then sit and wait for a response.

When he heard of the plan, Broadsword was livid, and told Edwards as much. "You've got to be kidding," he said. "That thing carries more guns than half the armies on Earth, and you want someone to fly over to say hello?"

"It's essential to make contact with it," Edwards maintained.

"We've *tried*. It's not interested. Apparently we have nothing to tell them."

"Nonetheless, Captain, I've been ordered to try."

Broadsword sighed loudly and shrugged.

"Okay," he said, "I'll go fire up the *Ark Royal*. Who am I carrying?"

"Two binary code experts. If anyone can talk to our new friends, they can. But, Broadsword, you won't be carrying them."

"What do you mean?"

"For some reason that escapes me, NASA considers you valuable. I've been told not to risk you on this mission."

"*What*?"

"I suppose they don't want to let our only Native American shuttle pilot get his fool head blown off."

"That is the most . . ."

Edwards interrupted him with a wave of the hand. "I'm sending Haggerty in the *Arizona*. He volunteered to fly the cipher men out to that ship."

"Haggerty is green. He's only been in space three months."

"Yes, but he's ambitious, eager to please and he volunteered. There will be no further argument on the matter."

"Do you mind if I talk to him?" Broadsword asked.

"Yes!" Edwards said, nearly in a shout. "Keep out of it, Captain! You were the first to recognize the goddam thing! Leave the rest of it to us!"

Of course, Broadsword couldn't leave the rest of it to H5. When the *Arizona* was about to cast off from docking bay 5, Broadsword was on the dock, watching and feeling uneasy. Broadsword didn't know Haggerty very well. Haggerty was older than he, recently transferred from the Air Force, and too much of a straight arrow for Broadsword's taste. He never spoke ill of anyone, shook every hand thrust in his direction and didn't question orders. He never drank, didn't smoke, was never seen to womanize and was, in general, exactly the sort of person Broadsword avoided. But there was something about that red-cheeked innocence which made Broadsword feel sorry for the man. Even if he couldn't do anything to help, Broadsword stood on the dock watching the *Arizona*'s cargo bay being loaded with antennas and broadband radio equipment.

By the time Haggerty arrived, looking like an Academy graduate in his clean uniform, the sense of futility was overwhelming. Broadsword shook hands grimly.

"Good luck, Jim," Broadsword said, forcing a smile.

"Don't worry about us. We'll be home in time for dinner."

"Just the same, keep your hand on the throttle."

"Sure," Haggerty replied with a laugh, not at all catching the seriousness in Broadsword's suggestion. He followed the two code experts down into the access hatch, and the hatch slammed shut behind them.

Broadsword watched the hatch close, then turned and walked off the dock. In less than a minute, the dock was depressurized and the *Arizona* launched and away.

The briefing room was filled with pilots, copilots, H5 technicians and administrators. H5 Control was using a portable setup there, and the huge viewscreen was alive with a split-screen image of the impending confrontation. Half the screen showed the alien warship as seen from the *Arizona*'s nose camera; the other half showed an overall picture of the shuttle approaching the gigantic ship.

Broadsword, Chambers and Baxter hedged around Leslie and her communications panel as the telemetry from the *Arizona* showed the alien growing larger by the minute. And the closer it got, the more Broadsword fidgeted.

"What's she making?" Baxter asked, nodding at the image of the *Arizona*.

"Ten thousand to a distance of ten miles. Dead slow afterwards," Broadsword said.

"Dead slow now," Leslie said. "They should start broadcasting soon."

As if on cue, the *Arizona* burst forth with a broadcast plea in English, Russian and three types of binary code for a face-to-face meeting. That completed, the shuttle broadcast television images of a stylized man, woman and small child. The man had his hand raised in greeting.

"That gesture is universal," Leslie explained. "It goes back to the ancient Romans. The open hand shows peaceful intent, because the hand clearly isn't holding a weapon."

"The Nazis used it, too," Baxter growled.

"The guys in that ship are never going to go for this crap," Broadsword said. "They know *where* we are, so they must know *who* we are. Those idiots at Arecibo have been broadcasting messages for twenty years, telling anyone willing to listen what we're all about. Our eagerness to call attention to ourselves has brought this on us."

Baxter still had his eyes glued to the screen as the great ship drew nearer.

"Those aren't gun ports along the sides, boy," he said. "They look more like docking bays to me."

"You could be right. Who needs gun ports with all the armament that thing carries on her decks?"

Despite all the messages from the *Arizona*, the alien ship made no reply.

"Why won't they answer?" Leslie asked in frustration.

"Why should they?" Broadsword replied. "They don't have to be courteous, not with power like that."

The *Arizona* was within a mile of the ship, which filled the entire viewscreen of the briefing room, and had stopped. For several long, pregnant moments there was no movement, and no sound. Then as Broadsword watched in horrow, a large gun turret located amidships turned slowly, its long and ugly barrel swinging toward the *Arizona*. Broadsword grabbed the microphone away from Leslie and yelled into it.

"Haggerty! Full ahead! Get the hell outta there!"

The picture from the nose camera suddenly blurred as the MBEs kicked in at full power.

"Oh, my God!" Leslie gasped.

The crowd in the briefing room held its breath as the telemetry cleared up once the *Arizona* picked up speed. The *Arizona* banked sharply to port, turning in close to the side of the alien, then shot down and away. The picture from the hub observatory showed the shuttle fleeing straight away from the warship as a pulse of light shot out from the cannon and missed the shuttle by a few hundred yards astern.

Edwards swore violently and clenched his fists so tightly the knuckles went white.

There was another pulse of light, which this time missed the *Arizona* to starboard.

"Haggerty!" Broadsword yelled. "They're lousy shots! Don't fly straight! Zigzag!"

The *Arizona*'s triple MBEs sent a brilliant trail of fire across the heavens as the space-speed indicator shot past twelve thousand miles per hour. Broadsword held his breath as his advice went ignored. The *Arizona* flew a straight path away from the alien battleship as the turret which had missed twice already zeroed in one last time.

"Haggerty!" Broadsword shouted, the words choking out of him.

The third salvo caught the *Arizona* in the engines. The radio emitted a stifled scream and the shuttle blew up. Then there was silence, as the picture from the hub observatory showed large and small bits of the spacecraft spreading out into space. Leslie buried her face in her hands.

Broadsword and Margot stared into one another's eyes. They were thinking the same thing, and there was no need to discuss it.

"Let's go," he said.

They slipped out of the room and were halfway down the inner rim corridor to the spoke where the *Ark Royal* was docked when Baxter caught up with them.

"You ain't goin' nowhere without me," he said.

The three of them hurried to the elevator, and before long were buckling themselves into the *Ark Royal*.

"I got it all worked out," Baxter said, taking the seat behind Margot. "There's a safe zone right along the gunwales. The top guns can't point that far down and the bottom ones can't point that far up. I'd say for the depth of the freeboard and maybe half a mile out we'll be safe."

"What about those ports?"

"Docking bays, boy, docking bays. They won't have guns in 'em."

"Let's hope not."

Margot ran the program for automatic launch, and the *Ark Royal* was away. As the ship pulled away from the station, Broadsword activated the radio.

"H5 Control, this is *Ark Royal*. Please listen, Leslie, and don't talk. Prepare for twelve channels of high speed telemetry, optical and standard sensor."

The reply was immediate. "Nathaniel . . . please come back! My God, what are you doing?"

Broadsword frowned.

"Check circuits, H5 Control. You're breaking up. I can't hear you."

Edwards' was the next voice on the radio.

"Broadsword, you get back here! That's an order!"

Broadsword switched off the receiver and pushed the throttles all the way forward. As H5 receded behind them, the alien warship loomed up ahead. It was still orbiting Earth, as if nothing had happened.

"Even overtaking her, I'm only going to have four or five seconds on target," Broadsword said. "I'm gonna run by her port side at fifty thousand miles an hour."

"That's more than enough time," Baxter said. "You can fire all six Rock Busters at once."

"Bad idea. I'll fire five of them at half-second intervals as we run up her side. I want one to keep in reserve for the trip home. Assuming we're going to have a trip home."

Margot was busy making computations and finally announced the results. "The best I can do with target programming is to set them for the fighting decks. There are so many goddam targets on that ship it won't matter much what we hit. Anything will do."

"Damn. I wish the Rock Busters were nuclear-tipped."

"It's a little late to think of that," she said.

Indeed, it was. The *Ark Royal* swept in on the warship from astern, sending back twelve full channels of telemetry all the while. As the shuttle closed the gap, the warship's two large stern guns trained on it.

"Here we go," Broadsword said.

The alien opened fire at one thousand miles.

"You've got maybe thirty seconds to fly through this flak," Margot said as Broadsword flew the ship like one of the fighter aces he so enjoyed watching on old movies.

The *Ark Royal* weaved in toward her gigantic adversary. The brilliant laser pulses seared by the wings, almost close enough to touch, but none of them struck home.

"Arm the missiles," Broadsword ordered.

"Missiles armed."

"That should give the bastards something to think about," Baxter said.

The *Ark Royal* screamed in at the warship then

and, as Baxter predicted, found a blind spot extending a half mile out from the port side. Broadsword fingered the firing button atop his control stick nervously and, the instant the *Ark Royal*'s bow came up on the warship's stern, pressed down hard on it. With mechanical precision, the five Rock Busters shot out from under the wings and impacted on the upper superstructure of the warship.

Several puffs of smoke and flashes of fire erupted, one of them on a gun turret. Small chunks of metal flew from the stricken turret.

The *Ark Royal* shot by the warship's bow and into open space once again.

"Get ready for flak again," Broadsword said as he made a sweeping turn back toward H5.

"They didn't open up until a thousand miles on the way in," Baxter said. "There could be a range limit to their lasers."

"That's too much to hope for."

But as the *Ark Royal* pulled away, there was no flak. Instead, from the blackness of one of the docking bays came a small fighter. A bit more than half the size of the *Ark Royal,* it was shaped like a symmetrical boomerang and was entirely black with no obvious markings. It flew with the narrow end forward and went straight after the *Ark Royal.*

"So that's it," Margot said. "They don't want their own man to fly through the flak."

"Good," Broadsword said. "It will give us a chance to see what their pilots are made of."

He put the *Ark Royal* into a tight turn. "See if you can figure out the range limit on this fighter's guns," he said.

Broadsword flew straight at it until it opened fire at 100 miles. A bright flash of light shone in the *Ark Royal*'s windows and a slight shudder went through the craft. "Got us," Broadsword said. "A bit, anyway." He turned to starboard and up. "So there's a range limit on it, too."

The Boomerang turned to follow the *Ark Royal*, and as soon as it was on his tail, Broadsword spun to port and down. As H5 and Kennedy Control watched on monitors, the two ships twisted and whirled in a dogfight of a sort that hadn't been seen on Earth in half a century. The alien fighter was slower than the shuttle and not as maneuverable, but its guns could fire one hundred miles while a Rock Buster was good for perhaps ten.

Swinging back and forth to confuse the alien's fire, Broadsword let the Boomerang move up on him and, in a sudden burst of inspiration, fired his retro engines. As the *Ark Royal* went into a screaming deceleration, the Boomerang overshot her.

"Now!" Baxter growled, and Broadsword pressed the firing button.

His sixth and final missile roared out from under the starboard wing and caught the small black fighter from behind. It disappeared in a hail of fire and debris which Broadsword avoided only by making a sharp turn.

"Nice shot, boy!" Baxter yelled. "Haggerty was a dumb fuck but I think that gets even for him!"

As Broadsword continued to turn, the *Ark Royal* once again swept within range of the warship's guns.

"Watch it," Margot cautioned. "They might not be so obliging this time."

Broadsword nodded and set a course back for H5. He switched on the radio and activated his mike.

"*Ark Royal* to H5 Control, returning to base."

Leslie replied, but nobody heard her. For all the docking bays on the port side of the warship suddenly opened, and from each came a fighter just like the one just destroyed. The twenty Boomerangs quickly formed up and flew right at the *Ark Royal*. He had forgotten to shut off his radio, and Broadsword had no way of knowing that half the world would get to hear him gasp, "Jesus Christ, it's a fucking armada!"

"I think it's time to go home," Margot said.

"No kidding."

Broadsword pushed the throttles full ahead and the MBEs roared with power. As he held the stick in both hands, twenty blips appeared on the Lower Hemisphere Viewscreen, which displayed objects below and behind the *Ark Royal*.

"What're we making?" he asked.

"Fifteen thousand. They're 200 miles back and closing."

"Hold on, everybody. We can't let them get within a hundred miles of us or they'll fry us like they did Haggerty."

"We're now making twenty thousand. They're 180 back and still closing."

"Kid," Baxter said, "we got to get some more Rock Busters in this thing, including a couple that fire backwards."

"I'll call in an order," Broadsword said bitterly.

"Thirty thousand," Margot reported. "They're 150 back and . . . hold on!"

"What?" Broadsword asked.

"They've started falling back."

"But still chasing us?"

"Yeah."

"They got a top end!" Baxter said.

Margot nodded. "Yeah, thirty thousand miles an hour."

"Then we're faster than them. More than twenty thousand miles an hour faster. We're faster and more maneuverable."

"Don't congratulate yourself too much," Baxter said. "Their guns are better than anything we got on this planet of ours, and we don't know how many of those little Boomerang fighters they got."

"I counted twenty," Broadsword said.

"If you think that's all they got, you're stupider than I thought."

"Are they still chasing us?" Broadsword asked.

"Yeah, but way back. Almost 500 miles now."

"We still have to land someplace. We can't run indefinitely."

Broadsword turned his attention to the radio one more time. "*Ark Royal* to H5 Control. We are being pursued by twenty enemy fighters. We cannot return to base."

The radio crackled and back came a familiar voice. It was Bailey, captain of the *Lexington*. "Shut up, *Ark Royal*," he snarled. "You've run this show long enough."

Broadsword looked into the distance ahead and saw one of the most beautiful sights he could imagine. Roaring toward him at full throttle, strung out in a formation five miles across, were the *Lexington, Hood, Constitution, Nelson, Concord, Exeter, Saratoga* and *Massachusetts.*

"The enemy's turning back," Margot said, peering at the Lower Hemisphere Viewscreen.

"Look at them!" Broadsword said, indicating the shuttles. "Every goddam ship we have in space!"

"I bet Edwards has shit his pants," Baxter said.

Broadsword stopped laughing long enough to get back on the radio. "*Lexington*, this is *Ark Royal*. Let them go, Dennis; I think we made our point."

Begrudgingly, the fleet of shuttles turned back and led the *Ark Royal* into H5. While two ships remained in space to stand guard over the station, the other seven docked. While flying back in, they'd used the radio to arrange a small victory celebration at the Sky Inn once they landed. But the instant Broadsword stepped onto the dock, he was met by Howard Edwards and two armed guards normally used just to police the antics of drunken miners.

"What's this?" Broadsword asked.

"You're under arrest," Edwards said, his voice barely controlled fury. "All three of you will be taken to your apartment and held there until I can arrange to have you sent back to Earth."

TWELVE

For twenty-four hours, Broadsword, Baxter and Chambers were shut up in Broadsword's apartment. The radio and television had been shut off, and only Broadsword's taped music kept them sane. There was enough to eat and drink, though, and they made the best of it. Looking out at the fabricated gardens of H5, Broadsword could detect no changes. People walked in the park and played tennis on the courts. Trams came and went as always, and now and then the appearance of new faces at the base of the spoke elevator told Broadsword that a ship had landed. Apart from that, though, the whole battle episode might never have occurred.

"That's what Edwards is trying to pretend," Broadsword said.

"What?" Margot asked.

"That the whole thing never happened."

"We'd be just as well off to pretend the same thing," Baxter said, putting his feet up on the coffee table. "They don't appreciate our riskin' our lives, so fuck 'em. I can tell you one thing, though. They're not gettin' me back on Earth. I'll jump ship first."

"Well, you'd better do it soon. There won't be too many chances once they stick you in a shuttle and aim you at KSC."

"I guess this shoots our mining scheme all to hell," Baxter said.

"Looks that way."

"On the other hand, given half a chance, I'll take the *Columbia* to the Belt and sit out this war."

"I guess it *is* war," Margot said.

Baxter laughed. "Darlin', if you can think of a better word for it, I'll bite. It's war, all right. I can't say I know what the hell they want from us, but their intentions are pretty clear."

"To be sure," Broadsword said. "Damn! I wish I could find out what's going on."

They lapsed into silence for a time, until even the silence became deafening. Broadsword was on the verge of putting on another music tape when there came a knock on the door.

"Here's our ferry back to Kennedy," Margot said.

"The first courts-martial in the history of the space program," Broadsword agreed.

But when the door opened, the man who stepped inside was neither Edwards nor one of his guards, but Admiral Jenson, smiling and with his hand outstretched.

"Admiral!" Broadsword exclaimed, jumping to his feet and taking the man's hand.

"Hello Captain . . . Baxter . . . Chambers . . . Good to see you."

Jenson helped himself to a chair.

"Broadsword, that was one of the finest bits of military flying I've seen in years. God, that stunt you pulled gladdened my heart."

"Does Edwards know you're here?" Broadsword asked.

"He does, poor fellow. He's been sacked, along with the entire H5 Council."

Broadsword's eyebrows elevated slightly, but he made no other response.

"I'm afraid you're stuck with me for the duration," Jenson went on. "Anyway, Captain, how did you find that trench down the side of *Armada?* Was it a stroke of luck, or did you figure on it being there?"

"Curtiss figured it out."

"Good show," Jenson said. "I owe you a box of Cuban cigars. I'll see that they're sent up."

"As long as I don't have to go to Earth to get them," Baxter replied.

"Never fear on that account. We need you right here. This looks like it's going to be a sticky one."

"Excuse me, Admiral," Broadsword said, "but you called the warship *Armada?* Where'd you come up with that?"

Jenson broke out laughing. "It's her new code name, replacing Haskins' Object, and it's *you* who named her, Captain, or did you forget?"

"I forgot," Broadsword said sheepishly.

"My God, that was funny. Do you realize that at the time you made that remark, about half the world was watching and listening via satellite hookup?"

"Don't be embarrassed, boy," Baxter laughed. "It beats all hell out of 'one small step for man.'"

111

"To get down to business," Jenson said, "the telemetry you sent back is still being gone over, but we have a few preliminary conclusions. *Armada* had to have come from another star system, of course. Which one we can't know, but it almost certainly is located within seventy-five light years."

"Why's that?" Margot asked.

"Wireless communication started in earnest in the 1920s, and the signals would now be about that far away. Most likely the ship came from a system within twenty light years, and was attracted to us by the deliberate messages sent out by various and sundry radio astronomers."

"Terrific," Baxter said.

"Agreed. It was always understood that anyone who might hear the signals would be more advanced than us. This is the result. Now, we have to find a way to get rid of those chaps in the warship. Your telemetry is being very helpful. For one thing, we know she's ion-driven."

"I thought that was just a theory," Broadsword said.

"It is, for *us*. They seem to have the process well in hand. You know the advantages and disadvantages of ion propulsion?"

"Slow acceleration and deceleration . . .

". . . and fantastically high top speed," Jenson said. "That *would* be necessary for interstellar travel. But the ship itself is slow and clumsy when it's not running at top speed. The way it is now, I think you could throw a rock at it and it wouldn't be able to get out of the way."

"Which helps explain all the guns," Baxter said.

"Yes, it does. It *has* to be a fortress. Which brings us to an interesting point. I don't imagine they built a warship ten miles long, carrying thousands of guns, just for our benefit."

"Meaning?" Margot asked.

"Meaning that they probably pay visits to inhabited planets as a matter of course."

"What for?" Broadsword asked. "To exact tribute?"

"That could very well be. I'm certain we'll find out in good time, whatever it is. Anyway, their fighters are ion-driven, too, but with, as you know, a top speed of thirty thousand mph and a rather casual turning radius. They're acceleration isn't astounding either, but there *is* one other thing—they're aerodynamically shaped."

"They can operate in the atmosphere?" Broadsword asked, astounded.

"Definitely. We estimate at no better than Mach 1.2, though, considerably slower than our best atmospheric jets. Why they might want to operate in the atmosphere is a matter of conjecture. They're not personnel carriers—far too small, assuming their pilots are roughly the same size as you and I. No, the Boomerangs are strictly one- or two-men fighters, so why they might want to operate in the atmosphere is open to debate. In any case, we estimate that as many as 100 Boomerangs can be maintained or manufactured in *Armada*."

"That doesn't give our nine shuttles much of a chance," Broadsword said.

"No, it doesn't. However, ten new shuttles are in the final stages of construction, and another twenty are being rushed into production. We're boosting the missile capacity to twelve and improving the missiles. We'll make that improvement in the *Ark Royal*, too, the next time you're on Earth."

"What about lasers?"

"I'm not crazy about lasers. They're bulky, and hard to aim. Rock Busters can track a target, and lasers can't. Besides, we know they're effective. You played a good deal of havoc with the upper superstructure of *Armada.*"

"Did I really? I thought so, but I was kind of busy at the time and didn't get much chance to look for damage."

"You completely knocked out one gun turret, destroyed two dish antennas and wrecked what looked like an observation deck. It wasn't the sort of damage likely to scare them away, but when taken with your outflying that fighter, it gave them a lot to think about. What you did may just have bought us the time we need to gear up for war. That flight of twenty fighters they sent after you *could* have engaged your shuttles, but turned back. Maybe it's just wishful thinking, but I don't think they expected us to be so formidable. Thank God I talked NASA out of taking the Rock Busters away from you guys."

"They wanted to?"

"Many times. You know, the old horse manure about arms in space."

Admiral Jenson finished his drink and stood. "I have to get to work," he said. "I'm having four laser and four missile stations built on the outer edge of the rim. There's plenty of room here for laser equipment, God knows. But until the gun emplacements are built, we're keeping two shuttles up at all times. It will be a four-hour watch.

Your next one is at 0700 tomorrow, Captain. Or, I should say, Squadron Leader."

"What?"

"I'm putting you in charge of the nine ships you have here, plus the *Prince of Wales* which I just flew up in. And the first new shuttle off the line will be yours, too. This is A Flight, and you're in charge. I said you'd make a good fighter pilot."

"But I'm not even in the Armed Forces," Broadsword said.

Baxter started whistling "You're In the Army Now," and Jenson grinned.

"As for you, Baxter, I want you to go on with life as usual. No trips to the Belt, but I'd like you to keep nosing around the Moon as you do so often. An essential part of our immediate strategy is to give the enemy the impression we're not bothered by their presence."

"Then everything will go on as before?" Broadsword asked.

"Yes. The same Moon flights. The same Earth flights. Everything will be the way it was . . . except . . ." He grinned. "I've cancelled the Opening Day ceremonies for H5."

"And after I went to the trouble to fly all that food and booze up here," Broadsword laughed.

Jenson went to the door and opened it. "Let me say one more time what a great thing you did, Broadsword. But if you ever take off like that against *my* orders, by Jesus you *will* be piloting the Staten Island ferry."

THIRTEEN

If Broadsword's impromptu assault on the alien warship bought time, it bought a lot of it. Several weeks went by, and *Armada* orbited the Earth without incident. Even with the best telescope on H5, it was impossible to tell if Boomerangs were coming and going, but it was generally assumed that *Armada* was running the same sort of fighter cover as H5.

The effort to turn H5 from a peaceful space colony into a military base proceeded without letup. Batteries of Rock Buster launchers were placed in the hub until the eight gun emplacements in the rim could be finished. The regular fighter patrol over H5 was discontinued when four automated missile launching satellites went into orbit around the station, their target computers directed to ignore targets bearing the transponder signals of NASA spacecraft. Anything entering that space without the proper transponder signal would be blown all to hell, but shuttles and experimental Earth craft were safe.

H5 had become the front line of the war against *Armada*. Moon colonies, although lying halfway between H5 and the orbit of the alien warship, were generally left alone. The Russian mining camps on the far side of the Moon and the American/European Space Agency colonies on the near were not given special treatment. The feeling was that they were peripheral to any designs *Armada* might have on Earth, and that any extensive attempt to beef them up militarily might betray the Commission's strategy of pretending that the presence of *Armada* really didn't bother anyone. There was one exception. The American mining and scientific base at Copernicus Crater was beefed up with guns, blastproof shelter and laser reflectors. But as the weeks dragged on and no further overt aggression was committed, lethargy descended upon Earth efforts. It was almost as if *Armada* had become a second satellite of Earth. There was a great feeling of relief at the lack of activity.

Through it all, Curtiss Baxter kept up his mining activities. Though he made no further progress in his efforts to get financial backing for a mine at Eichstadt, he did carry out mineral-hunting expeditions across the Moon's surface. As time dragged on, he expanded his search to the far side, which by tacit agreement was in the Russian sphere of influence. But Baxter had a couple of buddies in Russian Moon-mining circles and felt entitled to do as he pleased on their side of the Moon.

And so it happened that Baxter took the *Columbia* away from H5 one day not quite a month after the initial battle between Broadsword and

Armada and set a course for the dark side of the Moon. He made one orbit of the satellite, then landed at a site he'd long been meaning to prospect. It was on the west bank of Crater Tsiolkovsky, latitude 130° east by longitude 20° south. Baxter made a smooth landing, donned his EVA suit, picked up his mineral-detection gear and went prospecting. After two hours' poking around, he'd found nothing of value. Annoyed, he returned to his ship and took off.

Baxter flew north over the Moon's surface, crossed the equator, and continued on his way. He'd long had a hunch about the prospects at a small crater at 150° east, 40° north, and was determined to check it out. But while en route he flew over Mare Moscoviense, a large crater which was the location of a long-established Russian mining camp. Baxter had hoisted many glasses of vodka there and was tempted to return for another when, looking down from the vantage point offered by the *Columbia*, he saw two Boomerangs taking off from the strip adjacent to the camp.

Baxter watched the two small ships as they disappeared in the direction of *Armada*. When they were long gone, he radioed the base, but got no reply. Intrigued and a little apprehensive, Baxter landed the *Columbia* on the Moscoviense strip, suited up and walked to the base.

The camp, which normally had a complement of thirty men, was curiously devoid of activity. Several Moon Rovers, which normally would be scurrying about the surface repairing this, looking for that, stood idle in the fine, powdery dust. Even at times of least activity, Baxter could always find a few men to bore with his tales of missed coordinates and outraged colonial administrators. But this time, he felt more alone than he had in years.

Baxter walked from the strip to the main air lock and let himself in. The lock pressurized with a touch of the usual button, and he took off his helmet.

An acrid smell assaulted him, and he recoiled in disgust. He had only smelled burning flesh once, when he helped pull the remains of a Navy pilot from the wreckage of an F-14 at Kennedy Space Center, but it was something he could never forget. Baxter slipped his helmet back on and breathed deeply of his EVA suit's air supply. When his stomach stopped churning, he took a cautious step forward and opened the inner door.

The heavy steel pressure door swung open, and Baxter stepped into the Russian compound. The entry room was dominated by a circular desk surrounding a duty clerk's chair and a small computer terminal used for logging arrivals and departures. The entry room, and the rest of the compound, were as devoid of life as the cruel vacuum of space itself. Skeletons were everywhere. Each was laid out carefully on the floor, as if in repose. And around each, in the approximate form of an elongated tombstone, the floor was charred, with not even a speck of the ubiquitous Moon dust remaining. Baxter began a cautious search, taking his rough prospector's pick and hefting it, as if the killers weren't long gone. In the kitchen, two mess workers were similarly picked clean, and not even an ounce of meat remained in the stores. Baxter knelt by a skeleton. The bones were charred slightly but otherwise unmarred. Neither knife nor corrosive chemical had touched them. No technology that Baxter knew of was capable of performing such a ghastly feat. In an instant, the aliens' intentions on Earth were obvious.

Baxter continued his search of the Russian mining camp, looking for his friend Oginski, the Lithuanian mining foreman with whom he had hoisted so many glasses. Baxter knew there was something of the macabre in looking for one among so many skeletons. There was no easy way to tell them apart, and what good would it do to find the bones of his friend anyway? But Baxter did find Oginski, by going down the secondary branch shaft past the main microwave generator. He took off his helmet.

Once in the mining tunnel, he heard a slight whimpering. Baxter followed the sound through the semidarkness until he found his friend propped up behind a rock outcropping, deathly pale, with his breath coming in agonizing gasps. Baxter shifted the man's head from the rock wall to his knee.

"Sergei . . ." Baxter said softly.

Oginski opened his eyes and stared up.

"Baxter," he said with difficulty.

"I'll take you to H5, get you a doctor."

"Too late. Gas. Paralyzed, all paralyzed. Flesh-eaters, goddam flesh-eaters! I hid here, but too late."

"I'll have their heads for this, I swear it," Baxter said.

Oginski nodded with something resembling satisfaction, and Baxter held him while he breathed his last. Then he laid the man out in the stark chill of the mine shaft and returned to the surface.

Baxter went down the hall to control. The Russian computer labels were always a problem, but Baxter worked them out, bolstered by a growing sense of angry desperation. He switched the air filters onto high, making the air in the compound tolerable, then turned the radio link from the Russian frequency to that used by H5 Control.

He fitted himself with a Russian headset and tried the mike.

"H5 Control," he said.

There was for the moment no reply.

"H5 Control."

"Who is calling H5 Control?" Leslie's voice asked. For perhaps the first time, he was glad to hear it.

"This is Baxter calling from Mare Moscoviense. Get Jenson."

"Curtiss, is that you?"

"Get me Jenson, Leslie."

Less than a minute passed before the admiral was on the radio link.

"Baxter, what is going on?"

"I got the reason those bastards in the warship came here," Baxter said.

"And what is that?"

"They want meat, Admiral . . . *and it looks like we're it!*"

With *Ark Royal* flying point, the five shuttles swept around the Moon and, satisfied that no Boomerangs were in the area, circled Mare Moscoviense. While *Exeter* and *Constitution* continued to circle, *Ark Royal*, *Hood* and *Saratoga* landed at the Russian mining base, carrying a squadron of technicians and miners pressed into service as

122

pallbearers. Broadsword took *Ark Royal* to a landing adjacent to *Columbia*. Jenson, Margot and he pulled on their Flex Suits and rushed into the Russian base.

H5 technicians pored over the skeletons, taking samples of bone and measuring the tombstone-shaped areas surrounding them. Broadsword, Chambers and Jenson watched with a disconnected sense of horror. They'd had an idea what to expect, and the odor was gone by the time they arrived, so it was not quite the terror of discovery that Baxter had experienced.

It took the better part of half an hour for them to find Baxter. Jenson and Chambers had never been to the base, and Broadsword had never gotten past the main living area before. But Baxter knew the caves. He'd spent hours in them, swapping stories with Sergei Oginski and arguing the probabilities of ore discovery. They found him at last, sitting on the cold floor of the cave, staring blankly at his friend's body.

Broadsword knelt by him. "We're here. You have nothing to worry about now."

"Tell that to Sergei."

"I'm sorry about your friend," Jenson said.

"He was a good man. Great sense of humor, and imaginative, really could come up with some wild schemes. We were gonna do all sorts of things. He helped me with my claim, did you know that?"

Broadsword shook his head.

"Yeah, and never asked for anything in return."

"You're lucky it didn't happen to you, too," Jenson said. "Staying here the way you did."

"This has to be the only safe spot in the compound," Baxter said, getting to his feet. "It saved

Sergei from being cannibalized. They winged him, though...shot him with a hand laser, I guess. He died right after I found him."

"Cannibalized?" Broadsword asked.

"It may be." Jenson nodded. "The preliminary report from the technicians indicates some sort of device which strips bodies of all material readily convertible into proteins and carbohydrates. At least, my men can't think of another explanation."

"'Goddam flesh-eaters,' that's what Sergei told me."

"Couldn't a weapon do the damage we saw?" Margot asked.

"It would leave residue, and it wouldn't be selective enough to leave the bones. No, the flesh was *removed* and carted off, and if you can think of any reason other than cannibalism, I'll buy it."

"This is unreal," Broadsword said.

"There's something even more horrible, if you're game."

"Why not?" Baxter shrugged.

"The aliens didn't build that gigantic ship just for our benefit. The telemetry you sent back when you made your run on it showed battle scars which existed *before* you opened fire."

"Someone has fought them before?"

"And lost," Jenson said.

"You mean...?"

"I mean," Jenson said, nodding grimly, "that there's a chance we have encountered a race of beings who travel around this part of the galaxy, finding developing planets by listening for their radio signals, then ..."

"Eating them," Broadsword cut in, finishing the admiral's thought for him.

"Yes, I'm afraid that is a distinct possibility."

FOURTEEN

H5's docking bays had never been busier. With the ten spacecraft of A Flight being fueled and armed, the flight deck was filled with the hiss and steam of high pressure fuel and the metallic clink of Bloodhound missiles as they dropped into their launch tubes.

Broadsword looked down with considerable pride at the *Ark Royal*. Now fitted out with launchers for a dozen missiles, it was quickly being turned from an all-purpose spacecraft into a man-of-war. The Rock Busters were new—more maneuverable, with greater range and a larger payload. They were provided by the Soviet Union, which, following the alien raid on Mare Moscoviense, had thrown itself wholeheartedly into the war against *Armada*. In return, NASA gave the Russians its plans for the series 500 shuttles, and the Soviets quickly put ten of them into production. If Broadsword's squadron could hold out a while longer, Earth's fighter capacity would be doubled or tripled.

But Broadsword wanted to do more than just hold out. He'd talked Jenson into letting him lead his group against *Armada*, in a sudden attempt to stifle her ability to launch Boomerangs. Two weeks had passed since the Moscoviense atrocity, and the time seemed ripe for an assault. Broadsword's plan was traditional but effective. While the two newly built shuttles *Achilles* and *Alabama* helped H5 defenses keep watch over the space station, Broadsword would lead his flight of ten shuttles against *Armada* in five waves of two each. The attacking craft would fly down those trenches to port and starboard of the warship where her guns couldn't reach, firing ten missiles each. Each shuttle would keep two Rock Busters in reserve to use against the passel of Boomerangs expected to escort them home.

It was a good plan. The public, though it had been told only that the aliens had "massacred" the Russian miners, demanded revenge for that and for the unprovoked destruction of the *Arizona*. As Broadsword watched the last of the fuel pumped into the *Ark Royal*'s tanks, he felt Jenson by his side.

"Admiral," he acknowledged.

"Good morning, Captain. How do you like the new missiles?"

"I'll like them better when I see them impact in *Armada*'s launch bays. Until then, I'll take your word for it."

"I'll say this for the Russians, they had a lot more armament up their sleeves than we knew about. The new Rock Busters are excellent, absolutely first rate. The outer fin thrusters make them at least forty percent more maneuverable

128

than the old models, and the range! Well, it's not up to the range of *Armada*'s guns, but it'll serve you a lot better than what you've had."

"What about ones to fire backwards?" Broadsword asked.

"That will involve a modification of the targeting mechanism and is, as you can imagine, somewhat more involved. Give us two weeks and we'll have it. Damn it, Broadsword, when I was your age fighters didn't go fifty thousand miles an hour. Now, you blink once and you've passed the target."

"Believe me, I never expected to be flying combat."

"Neither did Curtiss. I'm having *Columbia* equipped with launchers for a dozen Russian Bloodhounds. I thought I'd let you tell him that he's now the first privateer in a few centuries."

"He'll fight with us," Broadsword said. "He owes his Lithuanian friend."

The *Ark Royal* was fueled and ready for launch. So were the other nine ships of A Flight. Broadsword climbed down into the captain's seat beside Margot Chambers.

Gauges and indicator lights glowed like diamonds across the cockpit. Broadsword recalled the many times on long cruises when he leaned back and pretended they were the lights of New York, and he was not far in space but walking down Third Avenue. Broadsword wiped away the thought.

"Ready?" he asked.

"Sure," Margot replied.

Broadsword slipped on his headset and switched the radio from Control to Fleet frequency.

"This is *Ark Royal* . . . A Flight check in."

The replies were swift in coming: "*Lexington*, ready." "*Saratoga*, ready." "*Exeter*... stand by, *Ark Royal*, we have a problem."

"I knew it," Margot said. "Things were going too smoothly. I should have known we'd never pull off a ten-ship launch without somebody screwing up."

Broadsword fingered his microphone irritably. "What is it, *Exeter?*"

"Granny's not feeling well this morning."

"Can you fix her up?"

"I don't know. Give us a while."

"How long?" Broadsword asked.

"An hour, I'm afraid," was the reply.

Broadsword tossed off his headset and climbed out of his seat. "I'll have to replace *Exeter*. We can't wait."

"It's only an hour," Margot said.

"Which means two or three hours, if they have to put in a new Granny unit."

"Jenson won't let you have either *Achilles* or *Alabama*."

"I mean to have *Columbia*," Broadsword said.

Broadsword found Curtiss Baxter sitting on a lounge chair on his terrace, staring at the simulated sky. In casual disarray around him were newspapers and books. A hardbound edition of *The Once and Future King* lay inverted at his feet. "You're feeling sorry for yourself again," Broadsword said.

"I thought you were flying today," Baxter replied, scarcely looking up.

"I am. *Exeter*'s out with a broken computer. I need you to fly with me."

130

"Not me, boy. Iv'e come to the conclusion I'm too old to slay dragons."

Broadsword was not about to be put off. "I need ten ships. I can't make do with less. Nine would throw my plan off."

"So fly with eight. Or get one of the new ships and have your ten."

"I can't do either. Come on, Curtiss...you promised Sergei you'd get even."

"That was before I got a chance to think about it. Attacking that thing out there ain't my idea of getting even. It's more like adding my carcass to the pile of bodies it's stacked up already. Believe me, boy, I don't mean to wind up my life as breakfast for some creature I've never set eyes on."

"You can blow *Armada* to hell and have plenty of aliens to set eyes on," Broadsword argued.

Baxter waved a finger at the younger man. "Don't get me wrong," he said. "I mean to have my revenge. But in my own good time and in my own way." Baxter put down his hand, then settled himself more firmly in his chair. "Get outta here, son, and go tilt at windmills."

Unable to think of anything further to say, Broadsword wheeled and stalked away. Ten minutes later, he was back in the cockpit of the *Ark Royal*.

"You didn't talk him into it, did you?" Margot said.

Broadsword shook his head.

"I knew you wouldn't. Anyway, *Exeter*'s okay now. The problem turned out to be a wire that worked loose in the NaviComputer. We can launch any time."

"I wish I understood him."

"I wished that once," Margot said, "but I learned better. Baxter is an original. Any man who leaves Earth and never goes back has to be."

"How could he turn me down?" Broadsword said. "I offered him the chance to avenge the murder of his friend."

Margot leaned over and gave Broadsword a peck on the cheek. "We have better things to worry about than why Curtiss does what he does," she said.

"Yes," Broadsword nodded, "we do," and prepared for launch.

A few minutes later, H5's docking bays opened and the ten shuttles of A Group spun off into space. Forming up in the traditional V with Broadsword flying point, they throttled up and accelerated to 50,000 mph. They would sweep around the Moon and come on *Armada* from behind, as Broadsword had done weeks earlier. It would be the most widely observed battle in history. All telescopes on H5 and telemetry from all of the shuttles were watching the assault on the gigantic alien warship. Beamed to Earth, the attack of A Group would be seen by hundreds of millions of viewers.

What wasn't seen was the quiet departure of ten Boomerangs from the far side of *Armada*. With all eyes focused on Broadsword's shuttle attack group, the alien fighters flew swiftly away from the scene of the coming battle and banked off silently toward Earth.

The Boomerangs didn't circle Earth or even come in at a low, sloping angle typical of Earth craft. Instead, they dropped nearly straight out of the sky in screaming dives not seen since the Luftwaffe was blown out of the air by the Americans,

British and Russians in World War II. Avoiding thereby the radar of the Atlantic Coastal Air Defense Identification Zone, the alien fighters pulled out their dive off Cape Fear, North Carolina, enduring G-forces that would have ripped an Earth ship apart.

They skimmed the wavetops and headed inshore, passing the Smith Island Lighthouse and heading up the Cape Fear River to the northwest. To avoid Wilmington, they left the course of the river to cross the broad expanse of Green Swamp, picking up the river once again near Acme. A few miles further, and less than three minutes after they pulled out of their dive, eight of the ten Boomerangs slowed to subsonic speed then began to circle the small North Carolina town of Beaconboro. While two alien fighters flew on to destroy the dozen F-18 fighters on the ground at the Fayetteville AFB a few miles to the northwest, the Boomerangs circling Beaconboro slowed even more and descended to rooftop level.

Without making a sound, they began to spread over the town a colorless, odorless gas.

FIFTEEN

Broadsword kept his eyes on the monitors as A Group swept up on *Armada*. They'd long since formed into five waves of two each, with *Ark Royal* in front and to port and *Lexington* flying alongside her. Unaware of events over Beaconboro, Broadsword held the stick firmly while Margot watched the ceaseless progression of Granny numbers.

"Two thousand miles, port and starboard in formation," she said.

His mind burning with the atrocity at Mare Moscoviense, Broadsword was an avenging angel, yearning for blood or whatever it was the aliens had flowing through their veins.

He touched his microphone. "At twelve hundred we'll break. Port column to port, starboard to starboard. Their reactions are slow, for some reason. Let's take advantage of it. Evasive maneuvers as directed until seven-fifty, when the two columns scissor. Scissor again at two-fifty, and good hunting."

The radio reverberated with agreement and

random chatter. Broadsword turned his attention to his copilot.

"What do you think?" he asked. "Are we a fighter force?"

"We'd better be," she replied. "Look at that."

Margot pointed at the target monitor, which showed a close-up of *Armada*'s stern guns training on the approaching shuttles.

"They know we're coming," Broadsword said, fingering the firing trigger nervously.

"Twelve hundred miles in ten seconds."

"Count down for the Group," Broadsword ordered, and Margot did just that, counting backwards as the shuttles sped up on the range limit of *Armada*'s guns. As she hit zero, the two columns broke left and right just in time to avoid the first salvos.

The brilliant laser pulses flashed by the *Ark Royal* and dissipated in the vastness of space. The ten spacecraft bobbed and weaved as Broadsword had instructed them, flying corkscrews around the warship's fire. While their laser pulses traveled with the speed of light, the aliens' aim was typically slow to react. Broadsword never gave them time to home in. As the stern of *Armada* loomed in the windows, the shuttles raced down the port and starboard channels, firing missiles automatically.

Puffs of smoke appeared along the ten-mile length of the warship. The Earth vessels wracked both her sides with fire, and debris was cast across the heavens. Shards of metal and plastic flew everywhere, and the ten shuttles had to fly through a hail of it. A hairline crack appeared in the right front window of the *Ark Royal*.

"Coming off her bow...right now," Broadsword said into the microphone as he put the ship into a tight turn to port and up. At the same time, the lead ship of the starboard column turned to starboard and down. When the two columns reformed outside the range limit of *Armada*'s guns, Broadsword checked the monitor for action behind.

"Keep an eye out for fighters," he radioed.

"They've stopped firing," Margot reported.

"Fighters any time now. Full speed ahead, everyone."

Broadsword pushed the throttle levers all the way forward. Once more the *Ark Royal* shuddered under the full acceleration of its three Multiple-Burn Engines. But still no fighters pursued her.

Broadsword studied the screen in disbelief.

"They're not sending anyone," he said.

"They're too far behind to catch us anyway," Margot replied.

"We're home free!" Broadsword exclaimed, touching the microphone once again. "*Ark Royal* to Group, any problems?"

"*Ark Royal, Hood* here," the reply came. 'Laser marks on right wing."

"Noted, *Hood*," Broadsword replied.

"*Ark Royal*, this is *Exeter*. We have damage on the tail section. Still maneuverable."

"Good work. You've had a hard day. Everyone else okay?"

Everyone else reported in okay, so the Group continued on a course which would take it back to H5. Once well away from *Armada*, Broadsword switched the *Ark Royal* onto automatic and gave a little shout of joy. Then he grabbed Margot and kissed her.

"We did it," he shouted. "We shot the hell out of them! It was like shooting fish in a barrel!"

"Yeah," Margot said, "wasn't it?"

"What's with you?" he asked, noting the sarcasm in her voice.

"It was too easy."

"Oh, come on. Not everything has to be hard."

"This should have been," she maintained. "But it was easier than when we did it alone. Their fire wasn't as accurate as before."

"We divided their fire. My plan ... remember?"

"I remember," Margot said, without enthusiasm.

"God, you're a worse downer than Baxter," Broadsword said.

But she was right. When the Group landed at H5 and Broadsword and Chambers were walking down the inner rim corridor to the briefing room, the atmosphere was deadly. Instead of congratulations and kidding, they were met with grim stares and silence. As the pilots and copilots gathered in the briefing room, even Broadsword's enthusiasm was dampened.

The feeling was confirmed when Admiral Jenson walked in, looking pale and drawn, wiping his brow with a handkerchief.

"Ah ... I saw the mission, and it was very good, very good," Jenson said, his voice faltering. "That was an excellent assault, Broadsword. We have evidence of significant damage to at least seven of the enemy's docking bays. ... I'm gratified to see there was no appreciable damage to our craft."

Jenson stopped talking long enough to fold his handkerchief into a pocket.

"What's the matter, Admiral?" Broadsword asked.

"There, unh, has been a problem," Jenson said, very reluctantly. "While the assault was taking place, a flight of enemy craft slipped away from *Armada* and...uhn...descended on a town in North Carolina."

"My God," Margot breathed, barely loud enough to be heard.

Jenson bobbed his head up and down. "The preliminary death toll is somewhat over four thousand," he said.

Beaconboro, N.C. was like many small American towns—quiet, dotted with elms and maples and white frame houses with azaleas on the side and the occasional hedge out front. It was quiet most of the time, but as Broadsword, Chambers and Jenson walked down one of its residential streets, it had the quality of a mausoleum. Even the song of a far-off bird or the mournful cry of a dog couldn't dent the heavy pall of silence.

For everywhere were skeletons. Mostly laid out in the street where they had been placed prior to stripping, each was surrounded by the same, tombstone-shaped bit of scorched earth as Baxter had found at Mare Moscoviense. A slight breeze off the Cape Fear River blew away the stench of death, but hardly the horror of the scene.

"It's like this all over town," Jenson said. "The aliens did all this with eight of their craft. Two others strafed Fayetteville Air Force Base, the only military air installation nearby. All in all, the enemy was in and out in less than an hour."

"Four thousand people," Broadsword said, as if in a trance.

Jenson nodded. "It's ghastly. Apparently they have a way of extracting the available nutrients from human flesh almost instantaneously . . . some sort of machine or ray. And it's not just human flesh. If you look at the skeletons, the scorched area around each is devoid of life. Even the microorganisms in the soil are gone, leaving a patch of Earth as barren as any on the Moon."

"Then they convert the nutrients into some compact form and take it back to *Armada?*" Margot asked.

"I would say so. We're dealing with nomads who are highly mechanized, so the fighter pilots can't just be feeding themselves."

"Cannibals," Broadsword said.

"Not really," Jenson replied. "They're not the same race as us, so technically speaking, they're not cannibals."

Margot grimaced in revulsion.

"I agree. The distinction doesn't give us much comfort. Anyway, we've got this whole town roped off, with access restricted to our people."

"It's my fault," Broadsword said. It was the first definitive thing he'd said since Jenson's auto had brought them to Beaconboro, and the others stared at him.

"What?" Jenson asked.

"What happened here is my fault. They used me as distraction. They let me get away with the attack on *Armada*. Better to let me take shots at them than to have me intercept the Boomerangs that did this." He swept his arm around in a great arc. "It's my fault this happened."

"That's nonsense," Jenson said. He would have said more, but was distracted when one of the soldiers conducting house-to-house searches of the block beckoned from a distance.

"Admiral Jenson, sir!"

"What did you find? A survivor?"

"No, sir . . . but one where the body's intact."

Jenson nodded, and the soldier went back inside the house.

"Look, Group Captain, if this tragedy is anyone's fault, it's mine. It was my decision to let you take your Group against *Armada*. From now on there will be no more assaults, at least not until we have enough shuttles to protect both Earth and H5 while they're going on."

Broadsword was unconvinced, but followed passively as Jenson and Chambers entered the house. The victim was a pretty woman in her early twenties, petite and with shoulder-length red hair. She was slumped over the kitchen table, her face resting on a booklet telling how to prepare a lobster for microwave cooking. Broadsword felt ill.

"There's no further point staying here," Jenson said. "I have to get back to the Cape for a strategy meeting. And you have to tend to your ship, Captain. The deuterium fluoride laser sent us by the Russians should be installed and ready for testing soon. With that and your special cargo, you have plenty to do, and you'll fly me back to H5 the day after tomorrow."

Broadsword was numb. He nodded perfunctorily and trudged off in the direction of Jenson's auto.

SIXTEEN

The old peach farmer's shack, long abandoned, stood by the side of a deep, swift-running stream which wound through the center of Merritt Island Wildlife Refuge. Broadsword sat on the grassy bank, wearing only jeans.

Broadsword had used the shack before, to escape NASA tedium and pretend he really knew what it was like to be a Native American. The shack and the stream were as sacred to him as anything. He had half a mind to stay there and never go back to Kennedy. Certainly there was some way he could support himself; by fishing perhaps, or maybe the peach grove could be restarted.

He was deep in these thoughts when there was the sound of twigs cracking under foot. Broadsword looked up in time to see Margot walking down the path. She too was barefoot, and wore cutoff shorts and a blouse tied under her breasts. Broadsword turned back to the stream.

"It may not strike you as any big deal, Adonis,"

she said, "but we're blasting off this planet in twenty-four hours."

"Terrific."

"I don't mind prepping the ship for you, but I'd rather not have to handle the entire mission alone."

Broadsword looked back up at Margot. She looked sensational. For perhaps the first time he realized how sexy she was. All that time spent alone with her, and he never really gave much thought to the matter.

"Go by yourself," he said. "You can fly without me."

"Jesus," she snarled, "you're as bad as Baxter. Two goddam prima donnas. What did I do to get saddled with both of you?"

Angry, Broadsword jumped to his feet. "I didn't ask you to come here, did I? You could have just stayed at the Cape and left me alone."

"Come on, Broadsword, be reasonable."

They were nearly the same height, and when he stared straight into her eyes he felt frustration, anger and need building like a storm inside him.

"Four thousand people are dead," he said, "and it was my fault."

"It wasn't your fault." She rested her hands on his shoulders. They burned like fire on his naked skin.

"Margot...it was. I got suckered into taking potshots at that thing while its fighters were wiping out an entire town."

"Your plan was good. You flew it well. Nobody expected them to pull an attack on Earth so soon. We all thought H5 would be next."

"An *entire town* was wiped out," he said.

144

"It would have happened no matter who was Squadron Leader," she said. "Damn it, you're impossible."

Broadsword was desperate. "Where do you get off being so goddam casual? Don't you see what's happening?"

"Sure I do. But I'm doing something about it. I'm flying that deuterium whatever-the-fuck-it-is laser up to H5 tomorrow. And the nuclear missile, too. No, Broadsword, I'm working on the problem while you're sitting by the banks of the Gitchee-Goomi feeling sorry for yourself."

Her tone was mocking, and Broadsword's temper flared. He grabbed Margot by the shoulders and squeezed.

"You're hurting me," she said defiantly.

Tears were in Broadsword's eyes. He didn't know what to do about anything. It was all spinning around him, out of control. Most of all he didn't know what to feel about her. She was in front of him, beautiful, saucy and wiseassed, calling him a coward. He loosened his grip on her shoulders, allowing his hands to slip down her arms to just above the elbows.

Margot's lips curled into a slight grin. She moved her hands quickly and the blouse came away. Her breasts jumped at him. Broadsword's breath caught in his throat. He had to accept the challenge. He grasped her breasts and squeezed them, his mouth pressing hard against hers. As his tongue swept her mouth, he felt her hands groping at his waist until she held him in her hand.

They broke apart and, out of breath, undressed and dropped to the soft grass of the riverbank. She was big, sweaty and bold; quite a change from Leslie's demure softness. Hoarse and anxious, they came together and she held him between her thighs, helping him move in and out, returning his whispers of passion until he spent inside her and she shuddered with him.

"My God," he whispered. He tried to pull out, but muscles within her held him captive. Broadsword opened his eyes and looked at her. She was defiant again.

"If you try to apologize, Broadsword," she said with a grin, "you're never gonna get your cock out of me."

Later on, they sat together by the stream. Both knew better than to talk about what had just happened. Finally, he leaned back onto the grass and stared at the sky.

"They say that Russian laser has a range of 2,500 miles," he said.

Margot nodded. "We can lie outside the range of their guns and fire at will."

"If it works," Broadsword said.

"Only one way to find out," Margot replied.

As the *Ark Royal* pulled away from H5 and Leslie's words of encouragement faded, Broadsword watched with considerable admiration as Margot laid in the course. She always was better at navigation than him. She could wade through the massive technology contained in the *Ark Royal*'s computers and panels with nary a pause. The talent seemed in opposition to the rest of her character, but she had it nonetheless.

"Okay, boss," she said, "the Granny numbers

are in the NaviComputer. We'll go in at top speed, taking her head-on."

"That ought to give them something to think about," Broadsword said.

"Yeah... a combined approach speed of somewhat over ninety-four thousand miles an hour. Their guns can't handle *that*."

"Let's hope not. I have to fly straight and level in order for the laser to work."

The deuterium fluoride laser, mounted on the nose of the *Ark Royal* just above and behind the retro engines, was said to be capable of punching a ten-inch diameter hole in half-inch thick steel at a range of 2,500 miles. If it performed up to par, there would be no need for Broadsword to get within the range of *Armada*'s guns. Just to be safe, the head-on approach was decided upon. It would give Broadsword but a ten-second period in which to fire the laser before having to break off and bank away, but all twelve channels of telemetry would be trained on *Armada* to see the result.

In addition, as the *Ark Royal* made its approach, Margot would open the cargo bay doors and deploy an Air Force Bedivere missile armed with a 100-megaton hydrogen bomb. It would be the first use of nuclear weapons in space, at least the first by an Earth power, but deemed necessary in the American-Russian-British strategy session held a few days before in London. Between the laser and the missile, the two most powerful Earth weapons, a test of ultimate power between Earth and *Armada* would be made.

Reaction to the Beaconboro atrocity had been worldwide and unanimous. The cries for revenge had become a torrent. The radio astronomers who had so diligently filled the heavens with messages of peace and noble intentions were treated as outcasts, and in several cases had to go into hiding. Churches were doing more business than they had in centuries, reflecting a sense of general despair which accompanied the widespread anger. Throughout it all, Broadsword and Chambers were held up as the heroes of the piece. Despite his fears, Broadsword was not blamed for Beaconboro, but remained in the public mind as the one who'd gotten pissed off and attacked the intruders very early in the game.

The *Ark Royal* swept out to the orbit of *Armada* and turned to fly down it, straight at the bow of the onrushing warship. The cockpit lights flashed like a thousand Christmas trees as Margot programed the targeting computer for the Bedivere missile. When the *Ark Royal* passed the ten-thousand-mile mark, a fleet of ten Boomerangs was launched to meet it. Broadsword had no fear of them. They couldn't be accurate at the approach speed at which they were flying. And their presence was in one way a good sign.

"They're worried about us this time," Broadsword said. "Maybe this means there'll be no sneak attacks on Earth."

Margot said nothing, for she was caught up in her computers. The MBEs roared and the *Ark Royal* shook as the distance narrowed. The distance-to-target indicator was nearly unreadable as the numbers changed violently. Meant for docking control, it wasn't designed for attack runs of close to one hundred thousand miles an hour. But Granny and the NaviComputer seemed to have a firm grasp on things, as they fed back *Armada*'s coordinates to Broadsword in firm, confident figures.

Broadsword peered through the window at the target. In books on military history, he'd seen head-on paintings of the World War II Japanese battleship *Yamato*, the most powerful such craft ever built. Her 18-inch guns could hurl a 3,220 pound shell over twenty-five miles, yet she was sunk by American aircraft off the coast of Japan in a brief battle. *Armada* struck him as very much like the *Yamato*, only a hundred times bigger. Yet the *Ark Royal* was at least that much superior to the best World War II fighter planes. Could the same feat be brought off half a century later in the dead of space? Broadsword decided it was possible.

Margot opened the cargo bay doors, and, silently, hydraulic mechanisms raised the missile launcher. The Bedivere was fifty-two feet long by three feet across and had the engine power of some early satellite boosters. Painted white with red and blue stripes, its leading edges covered with laser deflectors, the missile was specially adapted for use in space. That meant fin and fuselage thrusters rather than ailerons, and a somewhat more elaborate targeting computer.

Broadsword savored the view on the monitor which showed the Bedivere pointed down the throat of the mammoth warship. It wouldn't be long now before everybody knew where he stood.

"I've got ten Rock Busters targeted for those Boomerangs," Margot reported. "They'll fire simultaneously when we get within range. These are the second Russian ones. They're set to blow the shit out of anything that doesn't have a service transponder aboard. In other words..."

"We can just fire the sons of bitches without regard to aiming them. They'll blow up everything in the area but us."

"You got it."

"Why aren't we winning this war?" Broadsword asked. 'On paper, we have all the advantages."

"Let's wait and see what happens after this round."

The final approach to *Armada* was terrifyingly short. As the two forces closed ranks, the immensity of the warship was all too apparent to Broadsword and Chambers. Still, they switched on the telemetry and forged ahead, with but seconds separating them from battle.

Armada flew toward them, her phalanx of fighters soaring ahead. At twenty-five hundred miles, *Ark Royal* opened fire. For fifteen hundred miles, Broadsword raked the front sections of *Armada* with pulses from the deuterium fluoride laser. At twelve hundred miles, Margot fired the ten Rock Busters, which curled off wickedly toward the approaching Boomerangs. As Broadsword watched in fascination, seven of the alien fighters disappeared in puffs of flame and smoke, while of the three remaining Rock Busters one disappeared into space and two impacted on the port side of *Armada*, dislodging several armor plates.

"Coming up on missile firing point," Margot said.

"It's your show," Broadsword replied.

Margot nodded and fingered the firing button atop her control stick as the countdown indicator wound down to zero. Then she pressed the button and the *Ark Royal* was jolted by the launch of the largest missile ever fired from a moving vehicle. The Bedivere soared off ahead of the shuttle, spitting flame and accelerating beyond the capability of any manned craft built on Earth.

Broadsword put the *Ark Royal* into a sweeping turn to starboard, back toward H5. As all twelve channels of telemetry sent pictures of and statistics on the event back to H5 and Earth, Margot closed the cargo bay doors, and Broadsword pushed the throttles as far forward as possible in an attempt to clear the scene before detonation. There was no danger from shock waves, but Broadsword wanted to be well away from the radiation and the thermal pressures. Being the first man to fire a nuclear weapon in ten years was bad enough. Sticking around to watch it seemed especially immoral.

Ark Royal was ten thousand miles away from its target when the Bedivere impacted on the port bow of *Armada*. The explosion lit up a whole section of space. While there was no cloud, mushroom or otherwise, the debris of the detonation spread out from *Armada* and obscured it in a haze of flame and radiation which *Ark Royal* barely escaped.

"Jesus Christ," Margot said, and Broadsword pushed on the throttles until they nearly broke off.

When the explosion faded, the great warship sailed through safe and unaffected. The three Boomerangs not destroyed by *Ark Royal*'s Rock Busters were vaporized by the heat, but the mother ship sailed through unscathed.

"No effect," he said, "neither from the Bedivere nor from the laser."

"Surprise," Margot replied, rather acidly.

"The only thing that works against them is Rock Busters. Are we supposed to chip away at them forever?"

"Take us home," Margot said. "This is getting over our heads to figure out."

SEVENTEEN

The playback of the optical telemetry revealed little they didn't know already. *Armada*, which could easily be chipped away at with small chemical missiles, was impervious to nuclear weapons and laser fire. To be sure, the lasers left slight scorch marks on the external surfaces, but they did no real damage. And the 100-megaton hydrogen bomb appeared to have no effect whatsoever. As remarkable as it seemed, one tiny Rock Buster did more damage than the large Bedivere missile.

Jenson sat at his desk in the briefing room pondering these things. He'd long since moved his office from Edwards' old, windowless cubicle to the briefing room, with its glass ceiling and instant access to a view of the cosmos. Languishing in the front row of chairs were Broadsword and Chambers, fresh from their most recent run on *Armada*. Spread around the room behind them were the other A Flight pilots and copilots.

"The Bedivere detonated right against the hull," Jenson said, reading from a computer printout. 'According to all we know of structural materials, she should have been vaporized. She was not. Therefore..."

"We have a lot to learn about structural materials," Broadsword cut in.

"Precisely. The deuterium fluoride laser also had little effect. So our most potent weapons are of little value to us, and we're stuck with Bloodhound missiles. Unfortunately, using them it might take us years to destroy *Armada*, and we don't have the time."

"We'll have to destroy their fighters," Broadsword said. "Without them they'd be helpless."

"Presumably," Jenson said, nodding. "We could also send in the squadron to use concentrated fire on *Armada*'s engines, hoping to blow them up. However, they use ion power and our experts say that system of propulsion doesn't lend itself to being detonated by a lucky shot with a Rock Buster. Furthermore, I'm inclined to leave her engines alone, hoping they might get the idea to use them in departing. That's if we become enough of a nuisance to them, of course."

"In other words, Admiral," Margot said, "we have to leave *Armada* alone. We're stuck fighting a defensive war."

"I hate to say it, but you're right. For the time being, all we can do is pick off her fighters and defend the Earth. I've ordered all the Moon colonies with the exception of the large base at Copernicus evacuated, to reduce the number of places we must defend. Copernicus is in a natural fortification...the crater walls are steep enough to interfere with a Boomerang's turning radius... and is being armed with missiles and laser cannons."

"We have to sit here and wait for them to attack, with whatever they feel like throwing at us, is that it?" Broadsword asked.

"That's it," Jenson said reluctantly. "Of course, next week five new American and five new Russian shuttles will come off the line and go into service. The week after that, another ten shuttles will join the fleet. We'll have a total of thirty then . . . three squadrons . . . maybe we'll be able to come up with some new ideas to use against *Armada*."

Baxter's voice was unexpected and, coming as he walked up the aisle to take a seat between Broadsword and Chambers, something of a shock.

"It's the *old* ideas we should stick with," he said.

"Hello, Baxter," Jenson said. "I thought you were sitting out this war."

"I still might do that. However, I have noticed a few things, and if it won't mess up your carefully laid plans, would like to talk about them."

"Go ahead."

"What do you see about their technology?" he asked.

"Well," Jenson said, "it's pretty good, all in all. Better in some areas than others."

"Yeah, better in some areas than others. We're dealing with nomads, right? Attracted to the radio emissions of civilizations with maybe a basic knowledge of space travel?"

Jenson nodded.

"Well, what sort of weapons do civilizations like that have? Nuclear warheads and high energy lasers."

"Just what *Armada* is equipped to defend against," Jenson said, intrigued.

"You said it. We know they can defend against both, and they *use* lasers as offensive weapons. So what we got here is a bunch of clowns who have passed through the nuclear stage...no longer give it a second thought, in fact...and who think lasers are the epitome of warfare. Their best efforts are in advanced particle and beam weapons, right? Considering how fast it works, their flesh-strippers have to be beam oriented."

"Very good, Baxter," Jenson said, even more intrigued, "very good."

"Even their propulsion is by advanced particle...ion drive. So these guys are ready to make the big leap way into the future. But, they forgot one thing. While you're fooling around developing exotic weapons and propulsion systems, you tend to forget that a rock thrown at your head..."

"...can still hurt," Jenson cut in. "Yes, you're right."

"Our Rock Busters must be two or three hundred years out of their past," Baxter said, "but they still hurt. Not much, and it may take a lot of them to do any real damage, but the fact is we found a weak spot. There's another weak spot."

"What's that?" Jenson asked.

"They got a big tendency to regard things like Rock Busters as too small to worry about. There may be other things they don't worry about, either. Things we take for granted. I don't know what that might be, but then I'm just a lowly asteroid prospector, not a big shot military tactician."

"You're doing very well," Jenson laughed. "In

fact, I think you've justified my putting new missile launchers on your shuttle."

"They can defend against big weapons," Baxter concluded. "They can't protect themselves against small ones, and they can't seem to protect their fighters at all. Sonny Boy here..." Baxter gave Broadsword a poke on the arm, "...got seven kills his last time out, which is ridiculous. No, you can keep your nuclear missiles and laser guns. I'd fire a cannon ball at the sons of bitches if I could figure a way to set the fuckin' thing off."

Jenson laughed, as did several members of the squadron.

"And while we're on the subject of their fighters," Baxter went on, "I think that if you ─ ."

He was interrupted by the shrill rasp of a red alert signal. Originally designed to warn against decompression in the various vacuum-tight chambers of H5, it had been modified into an invasion alarm. Right on its heels was Leslie's voice.

"This is H5 Control . . . we have a red alert . . . enemy fighters approaching this station, ETA twenty minutes . . . I repeat, we have a red alert!"

"Goddamn," Jenson mumbled, as the pilots of the squadron ran for their craft.

Forty Boomerangs swept in on H5 from the dark background of space. Finally irked at H5's interference, the aliens had launched a major assault designed to knock out Earth's main military arm in space. With the station out of the way, *Armada* would be free to plunder Earth at will.

To meet it, Jenson sent up all the shuttles at his disposal—eleven in all, including the recently constructed *Achilles* and *Alabama*. The four slave stations orbiting H5 and armed with missile launchers and deuterium fluoride lasers were on full alert, as were the batteries built into H5 itself. As Broadsword prepared to command this vastly outnumbered fleet, he felt the heavy weight of history on his shoulders.

"I'm too young for this," he muttered to his copilot, who was fiddling with the targeting controls.

"You admit you're a child, then," she said, without looking over at him.

"If you admit you're a cradle-robber."

She looked at him, first in anger, then with a smile. "I'm entrusting my life to you, Broadsword, you better not screw it up."

He grasped the control stick as the launch countdown wound down to zero.

"Coming up on Fleet Launch," she reported.

Broadsword held on while the explosive bolts ejected A Group's eleven shuttles simultaneously. Once free in space, he pushed the stick forward and nudged the throttles ahead a little.

"This is *Ark Royal* ... form up on me. We're flying 3978 point 56 by 327 ... flank speed. You know the targets. We'll break off at twenty-two hundred miles and attack in twos. *Lexington*, on my starboard if you please."

The radio was assaulted by the gruff voice of Curtiss Baxter. "I'm flyin' your wing, Broadsword, nobody else."

Broadsword looked out to see the old, rusted hulk of the *Columbia*. He grinned and pressed his fingertips against his microphone.

"*Lexington*, you mind?"

"No," was the reply, "I'll find some way to amuse myself."

"You got my number one lady in there, Broadsword," Baxter went on. "I got to make sure she's safe."

"Tell him to get stuffed," Margot said.

"Form up to starboard, *Columbia*," Broadsword radioed. "When we get to the break point, keep with me and keep jiggling her around."

"I know what to do," Baxter replied.

"Flank speed," Broadsword announced, as the flight of twelve shuttles blasted away from H5 with all engines at full throttle. The forty Boomerangs were arching out of the sun, making them undetectable except on the instruments. The alien pilots had apparently learned something in the weeks they'd been orbiting Earth. Gone were the innocent strafing runs which presumed a lack of cleverness on the part of the victims. This time they approached at an angle which denied the Earth pilots visual confirmation, for no one could look into the sun.

Realizing the futility of a straight-on approach, Broadsword split his Group into two forces. They'd break to port and starboard, with the last four shuttles sacrificed to a straight-on attack. *Ark Royal* and *Columbia*, followed by *Prince of Wales* and *Exeter*, broke to port. To the right, *Hood, Nelson, Concord* and *Saratoga* broke to starboard, arching out thousands of miles before turning back on the original line of flight.

The battle broke out during what was mid-evening in most of the United States. It was visible throughout the country, with exhaust blasts, misses and detonations peppering the Earth sky with flashes of light. While the four shuttles approaching head-on maintained their course, firing

159

missiles as they saw fit, the ships of the wings crisscrossed, firing and figuring the best prospects for survival.

When *Prince of Wales* and *Exeter* had made their first run on the main force of enemy fighters and turned back for more, that portion of space between the Earth and the Moon was alive with artificial fire. *Hood* had taken a direct hit and blown up, never to be heard from again. *Nelson*, *Concord* and *Saratoga*, while they had accounted for their share of enemy fighters, were out of commission and drifting in space.

"We lost *Exeter*," Margot shouted.

"What happened?"

"She took two on the right wing and one in the aft fuselage! She's afire."

"Tell them to make it to Copernicus Base if they can. I got my hands full."

Three Boomerangs had split off from the main body of aliens to concentrate on *Ark Royal*. They flew in a tight V formation, with two fighters protecting the flanks of the leader. At a hundred miles, the two wingmen opened fire with their lasers, while the leader kept on coming, holding his fire.

"New tactics," Broadsword muttered, and fired three Rock Busters.

As laser bursts seared past his wings, Broadsword watched the enemy formation break up. The two wingmen banked out and away, while the leader turned down.

"They're testing the capability of our missiles," Margot said, still trying to clear up the blurred radio contact with *Exeter*.

If so, it was to no avail. The new Russian Rock

Busters roared through the heavens, tracking the two enemy wingmen relentlessly. The Boomerangs twisted and turned, but wound up as simultaneous flashes of blood and death. The alien leader was better off. The missile meant for him went wild, attracted by one of the many pieces of battle debris. Broadsword swore as it impacted, needlessly blowing up a long-harmless bit of drifting enemy fighter.

"They can be distracted by bits of debris," he said. "Radio that in to Jenson."

Broadsword nosed the *Ark Royal* down and after the alien leader, which was flying away from the battle, past the drifting hulk of *Exeter*. Pushing the throttles full ahead, Broadsword fired up another Rock Buster and went after her.

There was a flash of laser fire and a fist-sized hole appeared in *Ark Royal*'s left wing tip.

"Where'd that come from? Hey!"

"Behind us," Margot shouted. "There was one laying back."

"Goddam it, we've been suckered. I saw this in an old movie one time. Hold on."

He put the *Ark Royal* through a tortuous series of flips and curves, but without shaking the alien pursuer.

Finally, he snatched the microphone away from Margot. 'This is Broadsword. Somebody get this guy off my tail."

Slowed down by the evasive maneuvers, Broadsword watched the enemy gain on him at the same time as the alien leader was turning back. Broadsword roared past *Exeter*, dark and seemingly lifeless, with the pursuing Boomerang right on top of him, waiting for a clear shot.

A flash of fire from under *Exeter*'s left wing, and a Rock Buster raced up the enemy fighter's tail, turning it to fiery splinters.

"*Exeter!*" Margot shouted.

"Hold on for the other one."

Broadsword fixed his target on the fourth Boomerang, the one who had led him into the trap, and fired the missile.

The Rock Buster was fired at close range, and Broadsword just turned away in time. Still, the explosion filled the cockpit windows with blinding light. Broadsword and his copilot squinted, but turned back to join the battle.

"*Exeter* says you owe him one," Margot reported, the radio signal clear at last.

"I owe him that and more. Can he make Copernicus?"

"Yeah."

Rock Busters flew in all directions, some meeting their targets and others, confused by the many signals, spinning uselessly into space. Explosions lit up the darkness between Earth and Moon like a Fourth of July fireworks display. Broadsword counted twenty-two craft destroyed before he had to stop counting. He'd gotten four of them, and Baxter six. *Columbia* and *Ark Royal* stuck to one another throughout it all, even while *Lexington*, taking on two Boomerangs at once, was hit by a laser pulse from a third and disappeared in a ball of fire.

"Bailey . . . !" Broadsword cried out, too late.

Baxter was on the radio in an instant.

"You go after the son of a bitch that got him. . . . I'll take the two pricks he was chasing."

Broadsword nodded and spun the *Ark Royal*

into a sharp turn to port. As he did so, he saw the *Columbia* pull off to starboard, firing rockets from under both wings. As two explosions lit up the monitors, Broadsword pointed the nose of the *Ark Royal* at the fleeing enemy. Good old Baxter, he thought, vowing the same vengeance on the Boomerang ahead of him.

"Two hundred fifty miles and pulling away," Margot reported, feeding the coordinates of the Boomerang into the targeting computer.

"Not for long." Broadsword pushed the throttles as far forward as they would go.

"We're clear on all sides. No one pursuing or even nearby."

The enemy fighter curved away from the *Ark Royal*, speeding close to Earth in an attempt to use Earth's gravity to slingshot away from the faster shuttle. But Broadsword pushed his ship for all she was worth and soon the target loomed larger in his sights.

Skimming close to the upper atmosphere, the Boomerang raced toward a patch of space over Nebraska which the *Ark Royal*'s computers had long known to avoid. For unmindful of the conflagration around it, Solar Collector One went on beaming electricity to the ground, fueling the very television sets which showed the battle.

"We're gaining on her," Margot said.

"How many Rock Busters do we have left?"

"Eight."

"Fire up the next," he said, and she fed the firing information into the NaviComputer.

"I *want* that guy," Broadsword hissed, rubbing the tip of his thumb across the firing button.

"Me too."

"Is there anyone else around us?"

"No. Like I told you, we're all alone. We're coming around the Earth, Nathaniel. The main battle's on the other side."

"I just wanted to make sure. I've had enough surprises to last me the rest of my life."

Margot was fiddling with the Galactic Ranging And Navigation computer, and found a reason for consternation.

"We're getting a warning from Granny on the microwave beam," she said.

"What?" Broadsword asked, distracted.

"From Solar Collector One . . . you know."

"So what?"

"He's gonna fly right through the beam," Margot said, pointing at the image of the Boomerang on the targeting monitor.

"Who gives a shit? What's the distance on him?"

"Eighty miles and closing."

"I'll fire at fifty. Then we'll slingshot around and get back in the fight."

"If the fight's still going on," Margot said, making the appropriate adjustments.

The *Ark Royal*, shuddering all the while from the enormous thrust of her engines, closed the gap between it and the fleeing enemy. Ignoring the flashing lights and numerical indicators on the various panels around him, he peered out the windscreen at the alien ship.

"Seventy miles," Margot announced.

"I'm ready."

"Fifty-five."

"Hold on, kid," he said, and touched his finger to the trigger.

"Fifty," Margot announced.

164

But before Broadsword could fire the missile, the Boomerang suddenly burst into flame.

"What the fuck?" Broadsword swore as the *Ark Royal* flew through the expanding cloud of debris, and minute chunks of the destroyed enemy ship rained against the hull.

"Shit," Margot said as yet another hairline crack appeared in the windscreen. "We're gonna need another goddam piece of glass. The repair bay is gonna have a hernia."

"What was that all about?" Broadsword asked.

"She blew up," Margot said. "Maybe an old wound which finally got too much to bear. Who cares? Let's get back to the fight."

Broadsword shrugged, but remained bitter. "I wanted that one," he said, "for *Lexington*."

"We're in the microwave beam," Margot said.

Broadsword nodded disinterestedly and put the *Ark Royal* into a turn which would bring it around the Earth and back to the scene of the battle. It took only a few minutes to get there. When that sector of space hove into view, the sight made Broadsword's heart stop.

Lexington, Hood, Achilles and *Alabama* were gone. *Exeter* was making its way to Copernicus Base, seriously damaged. *Nelson, Concord, Saratoga, Prince of Wales* and *Massachusetts* were dead in space. *Constitution* was limping back toward H5, her main engines gone, using thrusters for propulsion. *Columbia* was nowhere to be seen.

Off in the distance against the starfield, half-a-dozen Boomerangs were returning to *Armada*, their job done. Of the twelve shuttles which set out against them, only *Ark Royal* had come through unscathed. Thirty-four of the enemy were

165

gone, but their purpose had been served. Broadsword's squadron was decimated.

Moreover, H5, which but recently was an example of the finest environment Earth could produce in space, lay a dead, smoldering ruin.

EIGHTEEN

Broadsword cruised slowly through the battle-field, looking in stunned disbelief at the bones of Earth defenses. The four slave stations orbiting H5 were blown to bits, and the gun emplacements on the rim of the station itself gone. Two of the five spokes were cut apart by laser fire, and the one sector of the rim which was almost, but not quite, opened to colonization was blown apart. Depressurized, the gardens and parks were gone; the plants exploded from within when suddenly thrust into the vacuum of space.

The electric trams which carried passengers in and out of the living and working complexes were adrift, useless. Broadsword's beloved tennis courts were reduced to rubble, and his apartment a mausoleum wrapped in a vacuum. Only the safe areas remained habitable—the travel tubes, elevators and the top floors of the Tower, where H5 Control was headquartered.

As the *Ark Royal* pulled up to H5, an expanding cloud of smoke poured from one of the spokes.

Broadsword and Chambers were silent during the approach. *Constitution* was all right, and with a bit of work on her MBEs she would be able to tow those other shuttles which still had life aboard them to either H5 or the Moon. Unable to raise H5 Control, Broadsword took the *Ark Royal* into bay 7 making a manual landing and, for the first time, doing it perfectly.

Margot tried without success to raise the longshoremen on the radio, then followed Broadsword to the exit tube.

"I hope the dock's pressurized," Broadsword said.

Margot punched a few buttons on the sensor array adjoining the hatch.

"It is," she replied.

The hatch swung open, and the stench of burnt insulation filled the *Ark Royal.* Off in the distance were men's voices and the sound of fire equipment. The two exchanged glances and pulled themselves up onto the dock.

The foreman of docking bay 7, wearing an asbestos jump suit over his normal blue work clothes, ran up, carrying a small extinguisher.

"How bad is it?" Broadsword asked.

"Bad enough. We've got electrical fires in bays 5 and 9, and complete depressurization in spokes A, B and C."

"How's the rim?"

"Shot to hell," the man said. "You'll have to use the safety corridors. What's it like outside?"

"Only *Exeter* and *Constitution* are still spaceworthy, and they're damaged. *Columbia* is missing. What about the spoke elevator?"

"Power just came back on. It's okay to use. Only goes to the inner rim level, though."

Broadsword nodded grimly, and the foreman hurried off down the spoke in the direction of bay 5. As Broadsword and Chambers rode the elevator to the rim, the lights inside the car flickered and the winches made ominous squeals. When they arrived at the inner rim level, they paused to look out the window at the devastation of sector one.

Everywhere were ruins. The apartment complex in which Broadsword had lived was cut apart by laser beams, one wall sliced open, laying the rooms bare. All across the public grounds, corpses lay in grotesque deformity, exploded like deep sea fish when they're pulled from the ocean bottom. In the outer rim wall, a hole big enough to fly a shuttle through was cut in the space formerly taken up by the Sky Inn. Margot looked away from the window in dismay.

"Let's go to the briefing room," Broadsword mumbled.

They walked quickly along the corridor, stepping over the legs and arms of wounded H5 technicians being attended to by hard-pressed medics. The sickening smell of ether replaced the stench of burning cables, and the bodies continued to mount as they neared the top floor Tower briefing room. In the room were two dozen persons, technicians and administrators for the most part, sitting in varying states of shock.

Several young women were crying, and when Leslie looked up from her radio panel and saw Broadsword, she ran to him.

Broadsword clasped his arms around her.

"Nathaniel... I was so worried! I didn't hear from you!"

"I tried to call, but you're not receiving."

"We are now. They got communications going again. We still can't raise Earth, but... God, just hold me!"

Broadsword hugged her in silence, until Margot finally interrupted them.

"Really, children, you're getting embarrassing."

Leslie broke away, and scowled at her antagonist. 'Is this more embarrassing then chickening out in the middle of the battle?"

"What do you mean?" Margot asked.

"Your boyfriend ran off when things got too hot," Leslie said.

"Curtiss? Where is he, anyway? I expected he'd beat us back."

"He's gone... chickened out, like I said."

"Leslie," Broadsword said, "you can't be serious."

"I'm afraid she is, old boy." The voice belonged to Admiral Jenson, who'd just walked over, looking many years older but still in command. "Baxter turned tail and fled right after you went after the enemy fighter that got *Lexington*."

"I don't believe it," Broadsword said. "I saw him get the two Boomerangs he was after."

"He got those, but three others got onto his tail. He sailed straight off into space and kept on going, even after they turned away."

"Maybe," Margot said tentatively, "they destroyed him. Or damaged *Columbia*."

Jenson shook his head. "They didn't fire a shot. He pulled away from them and kept on going. He disappeared in the direction of the Asteroid Belt. I'm afraid he's living up to his threat to fly to the Belt and sit out this conflict."

"We tried to call him back," Leslie said. "But he dropped off the sensors, and then communications were knocked out."

Margot walked to the vast windows lining the walls and ceiling and peered out at space. *Constitution* was limping into bay 2, and all along the rim pieces of exterior plating drifted aimlessly. And in the distance, another shuttle approached the station.

"That could be him," she said softly, not believing it.

Jenson and Broadsword joined her at the window. Leslie was already back at her radio console.

"Dixon," Jenson ordered, "find out who that shuttle is."

"H5 to approaching shuttle, please identify." Her voice echoed softly in the room. The reply came in an instant.

"Hello, H5 ... *Exeter* here."

"Well I'll be damned," Jenson exclaimed, "he's got her working again."

"What's your condition, *Exeter?*" Leslie asked.

"I got one engine running, and thought I might pop in to see if you chaps need some help."

"Ask him how he did it," Broadsword said, and Leslie complied.

"My old man always told me that when something mechanical goes wrong, to give it a good whack. I went back to the engine compartment and gave her a kick in the slats. It started right up ... one of them anyway."

171

A ripple of light laughter went through the room.

"It's good to have something to laugh about," Jenson said. "All right, Dixon, have him dock at bay 1."

"That leaves us with three ships," Broadsword said.

"Yes," Jenson said, "but that will do, unfortunately."

"That will do for what?"

"To evacuate this station, of course. We can't stay here. H5 is now the proverbial sitting duck. Earth is too far, and *Constitution* and *Exeter* in no condition for reentry. No, we'll have to move everyone to Copernicus. Her defenses are still intact."

"We can't move that many people in three shuttles . . . at least not in one trip."

"There aren't that many to move," Jenson replied. 'When the battle started, we had a complement of 160 on H5. I'm afraid there are less than three score left, and a third of them are wounded."

"We lost over one hundred?" Broadsword exclaimed.

"Most of them when the living sector decompressed," Jenson nodded.

"My God!"

"So we'll have to move all sixty in *Ark Royal, Exeter* and *Constitution*. It will mean setting up the cargo bays for passengers."

"If it has to be done," Broadsword said.

Jenson clapped Broadsword on the arm. "We'll muddle through somehow. I'll go have the shuttles set up for passengers."

Jenson started off, then turned back, his lips

curling into an ironic grin. "Oh, by the way, just before the battle we received a routine notice from Kennedy. It seems the chaps at Arecibo have suspended indefinitely their messages broadcast to other star systems telling them where we are."

"Terrific," Broadsword said.

He turned back to Margot, and slipped an arm around her waist. She was still staring blankly at space, the suggestion of tears in her eyes.

"I can't believe he's gone," she said.

"Curtiss will come back," Broadsword said softly.

"To what? A coward's reception? Damn...he's out there someplace, hiding. And I was just getting fond of the bastard."

"Hey," he said, with false cheeriness, "is this the tough broad I work with?"

Margot wheeled at him. "Fuck off, Tonto," she snapped, "and leave me alone!"

NINETEEN

Unlike H5, Copernicus Base was purely functional. A mining and scientific colony, it sat on a broad plateau near the center of the fifty-six-mile-wide crater. A runway built across the crater floor and up the 2.3-mile-high slope of the north wall allowed shuttles to take off without vertical thrusters. The base itself was much like H5 in layout, with a large central glass dome and recreation area and five spokes running off to smaller domes connected by semicircular corridors.

Copernicus Base was evacuated following the Mare Moscoviense atrocity, but in recent days Jenson had moved a skeleton crew back in to man the guns. Missile launchers lay around the perimeter, and there were robot emplacements at four points on the crater walls. At the top of the central dome, a fast-revolving laser turret had been constructed. From it, a gunner could have a complete sweep of Copernicus.

Ark Royal, Exeter and *Constitution* pulled into Copernicus four hours after the end of the battle.

H5 had been evacuated in record time and abandoned, to spin uselessly in its orbit. From then on, Earth's only outpost in space was Copernicus. As Broadsword lowered the skids and let *Ark Royal* slide down the runway of fine Moon dust, he felt a sense of futility. H5 was destroyed. Many of his friends were dead. Baxter had run off God-knows-where, and Margot wasn't talking to anyone. Worst of all, Broadsword knew that while Copernicus was a much better fortress than H5, it would still be hard to defend against an all-out attack.

Copernicus had five docking bays, one between each of the spokes. Shuttles docked head-in, to be turned around later for launch. Broadsword guided the *Ark Royal* into bay 3 and hurried away, leaving Margot to discharge passengers and shut down systems.

He helped Leslie out the exit tube and onto the dock. She had with her a large briefcase packed with code books and computer printouts. Even in the slight gravity of the Moon it was heavy, and Broadsword took it from her.

"I got it. You'll have enough to do setting up."

"Thanks, darling," Leslie replied, giving him a kiss on the cheek.

They started away from the dock, but Leslie held back, looking at *Ark Royal*.

"What's the matter?" he asked.

"Margot...I'm kind of sorry for what I said. Maybe I should tell her."

"Leave her alone for a while," Broadsword advised.

"I didn't have to blow up like that. It's just that she makes me really mad."

"Margot has a big mouth. She'd be the first to

admit it. Come on, Leslie, let's go set up communications. You can apologize when she's calmed down."

Leslie sighed and forced a smile. "I guess I'm really jealous of her for spending so much time with you."

"It's not very romantic in a shuttle cockpit," Broadsword said, giving Leslie a reassuring pat on the ass. "Besides, we're just friends."

"That's all? That's really all?"

"We'll never be more than that," Broadsword said, a bit ruefully. "I'm sure of it."

"I feel much better now," Leslie said, and headed down the spoke toward the central dome, with Broadsword tagging along behind carrying her briefcase.

The dome covered what passed on Copernicus for a recreation and meeting area. There was a circular bar, a large videoscreen, and a number of gaming tables. The floor was carpeted and set here and there with comfortable chairs and sofas. The ceiling was entirely glass and made for a spectacular view of the starfield and Earth rising above the crater walls.

From the center of the room, a spiral staircase wound up thirty feet before disappearing into the small room housing Copernicus Control. Set in the very top of the dome, it was a small communications booth with nothing above it but the newly constructed laser turret, reachable by a plain metal ladder. Unlike the reasonably luxurious H5 Control, this was nothing more than a radio room cramped and packed with equipment, some of it inching up the glass top of the dome.

By the time Broadsword and Dixon reached the

dome, it was taken up largely by pallets for the wounded. They picked their way through this impromptu hospital and went up the stairs to Copernicus Control. A gunner, pressed into service as a radio operator while the evacuation craft were landing, gratefully handed control over to Leslie.

"You can have it," he said. "I wasn't cut out for this many wires and buttons."

"Does everything work?" she asked.

"I think so. Granny's set on automatic sweep. She picked up the three of you coming in easily enough, and ranged you right down onto the ground."

Uninterested in the technology he found himself surrounded by, Broadsword climbed up to the turret and tried the sights on the cannon.

"You know how to work that?" the man called up.

"Yeah."

"You can relieve me for a while. I have to take a leak."

"Whatever you say," Broadsword replied, descending the ladder and leaning against the console next to Leslie. She was busy programing the computers to her taste and trying out the various pieces of equipment.

"Oddly enough, everything seems to work," she said. "The link to Kennedy is on. Telemetry on *Armada* is working..."

"Will we be able to see their fighters taking off?"

"No. This stuff isn't much better than what we had on H5. I couldn't pick them up that far away there, and I won't be able to do it here. I might

178

be able to spot them four hours out, using manual sweep, but that's awfully hard to do."

"You'll manage," Broadsword said.

"And, of course, when they're eclipsed by the Earth..."

"Nothing. I get the picture."

"Manual sweep is *hard*, Nathaniel. Maybe you should try it."

"Not me, babe...I don't go for all this lights-and-buttons bullshit."

"If you can run the laser you can run this," she said, tapping a manicured fingernail on the large, radarlike viewscreen which showed the Earth, Moon and the region of space around them. "All you have to do is...look, here's some debris from the battle."

She pressed her finger against the screen where several dozen points of light were suddenly illuminated by Granny's ranging beams. "That's all small stuff there, caught in Earth's gravity and being pulled down."

"And flying in formation," Broadsword said, bending closer to the screen.

Leslie was punching buttons and reading the figures which appeared on a nearby monitor.

"Velocity, thirty thousand," she reported, "steep angle relative to Earth...there's about forty of them in all."

"Get Jenson," Broadsword snapped.

"Where's the intercom?" she said, fumbling around the console. "Oh, here...got it." She spoke into the microphone which projected from the console on a steel gooseneck. "Admiral Jenson to Copernicus Control. I repeat, Admiral Jenson to Copernicus Control."

"Can you get me a point of entry?" Broadsword asked.

"Unh . . . yeah . . . just a second." More lights flashed and more numbers adorned the monitor.

"North Atlantic area . . . I can't be more specific just yet."

"ETA?"

"A bit under an hour before they hit the atmosphere."

"Well," Broadsword said, "it's better than nothing."

"What's better than nothing?" Jenson asked, crowding into the radio room with them.

"An hour's warning," Broadsword said.

"Not again!"

"Yes, but not us this time. Earth again, North Atlantic area."

"My God! Will it never end?"

"Just a moment," Leslie said, studying the figures on the monitor. "Yes, I think I have it. About 50° north, and around zero to 15° west."

"The U.K." Jenson exclaimed. "Leslie, can you put me straight through to Jodrell Bank?"

"Sure."

"Kennedy first, then Jodrell Bank."

As Leslie made the arrangements, Jenson looked angrily at the sky.

"There's nothing I can do," Broadsword said. "I'd never come near to catching up with them."

"You can sit this one out, Captain," Jenson said. "It will have to be handled on Earth, in the old-fashioned way."

TWENTY

The forty Boomerangs dropped from the sky a few miles off Stoke Fleming, leveled off above the wavetops, then flew up the Channel on a heading equidistant from Southampton and Cherbourg. They bypassed a large fleet of yachts on the first leg of the Fastnet race, then left the Bill of Portland several miles to port while turning slightly toward the center of the Channel. When they passed St. Catherine's Point, Isle of Wight, thirty of the alien ships climbed abruptly to forty thousand feet, while the remaining ten held to their altitude, dropping to subsonic speed.

When the thirty climbed so suddenly, they went on radar screens up and down the English channel. At Selsey Bill and Brighton, at Barfleur and Dieppe, coastal radar, warned to expect a sudden incursion of fast-moving small craft, found what they expected. Sensors aboard the aircraft carrier U.S.S. *Enterprise*, steaming away from a weekend leave in Portsmouth, lit up like the lights on Leslie's console. Thirty F-18s were sent up to intercept the Boomerangs, as were forty F-18s from the R.A.F. base at New Romney and twenty Mirages from the French airfield at Le Havre.

Off Beachy Head, the enemy turned north, setting course for London, across the East Sussex countryside. The reaction was predictable. The air forces of three nations closed on them at high speed. The Mach 1.2 Boomerangs were no match speedwise for the Mach 3 F-18s and Mirages. But they could climb, and did so—quickly moving to one hundred thousand feet, above the altitude capability of the air-breathing fighters.

The battle began ten miles offshore and over eighteen miles high, and went on the better part of half an hour. Firing from a distance of several miles and in extremely thin air, the Earth fighters found their missiles woefully lacking in accuracy. The Boomerangs, on the other hand, could operate as far from Earth as they liked, and while the range of their lasers was somewhat restricted in the atmosphere, they proved deadly accurate. What the aliens couldn't do against the *Ark Royal* they could against conventional jets. Laser pulses flashed through the afternoon skies, leaving great white streaks of vaporized water particles up and down the atmosphere. Vapor trails from the missiles arced upwards toward the invaders who, though outnumbered three to one, made a good showing for themselves. In the weeks since *Armada* arrived at Earth, her pilots had learned a great deal about tactics on the planet. They had, after all, learned how to distract men's attention from the true goals of their attacks.

For even as the thirty Boomerangs were readying to meet the Earth forces, the ten who had remained at wavetop level turned north up the Solent toward Portsmouth. There, unaware of the great air battle a short distance away and no longer protected by fighters from New Romney, 18,456 soccer fans had gathered to see a practice match between the Bitterne Sea Lions and the Reading Giants. Flying low over the Southampton docks, the Boomerangs slowed nearly to a halt, then circled the stadium.

For Captain Jonathan Fyfe, leader of R.A.F. Blue Squadron, New Romney, the day had been long and hard and would get worse. For some weeks he'd been itching to get into the war against *Armada*. Long on the top of the list of R.A.F. pilots qualified for shuttle duty, his chances to get into space had been doused when the ten shuttles originally assigned by NASA to the European Space Agency went instead to the Soviet Union. The war was threatening to be an American and Russian one, with no further British pilots likely for selection. And the C in C a British admiral at that!

To make things worse, when the alert came on the enemy attack, Fyfe's F-18 *Sky Diver* was in for repair and there were no replacements. He had to lead his men into battle flying a rather lumpy Girardeaux Outrider, a VTOL which could land on a dime but had few other advantages. Forced to watch the fray from his altitude ceiling of sixty thousand feet, Fyfe regarded himself the unluckiest man on the Earth or off it. When the extraordinarily long battle was over, Fyfe ordered his squadron straight back to New Romney with but the customary exchange of good-byes and thank yous with the American and French pilots. Fyfe had his mind set on a few pints and nothing else.

So the second alert came as a shock.

"Blue and Red Squadrons, this is New Romney," the radio said.

"Blue here," Fyfe replied, and listened while Red Leader responded in kind.

"Report, Blue Leader."

"Enemy destroyed," Fyfe said, in an almost lackluster manner. "We've lost three planes and Red five. The Yanks lost seven and the French, two."

"Understood, Blue Leader. Can you take on another assignment?"

"Negative, New Romney . . . we've flown an hour on afterburners. Everyone's nearly out of petrol."

"What about *your* plane, Captain?" the tower asked. "How is your fuel supply?"

Fyfe was caught off guard, and had to check the gauges. "Unh . . . I'm all right, New Romney. What's up?"

The radio was silent for several long seconds while Fyfe wracked his brain to figure out what the hell had gone wrong *now*.

"Blue Leader," the reply came, "break off and investigate reports of several enemy planes over Southampton."

Fyfe was stunned. "New Romney, I'm armed only with 50-millimeter cannons."

New Romney seemed unimpressed. "Confirm the order, Blue Leader."

"Confirmed," Fyfe said. After handing control of the squadron over to his second-in-command, he banked off to port and set a course along the East Sussex shoreline for Southampton. It wasn't a long flight, and he spent the time charging his guns and wondering what the devil use they would be against lasers. The Outrider was designed for close air-ground support in jungle or mountainous areas, not fighting alien invaders with exotic weapons.

Fyfe swept in over the marshes near Bognor Regis and crossed the various bays and inlets surrounding Portsmouth. As he neared Southampton, his radar picked up ten targets over the Bitterne section, climbing rapidly. All commercial and private traffic had been grounded, so the blips had to be the enemy. Fyfe shoved the throttles all the way forward, feeling both eagerness and apprehension. It was his chance to get into the war, and also a neat way to get his head blown off. I might as well throw golf balls at them, he thought, as the targets grew larger in front of him.

The ten Boomerangs rose from the ashes of their victims, climbing rapidly. Fyfe saw them strung out one after the other, as if a caravan, the last few seeming sluggish, perhaps heavy. The lead fighters were at sixty thousand and climbing, out of his reach. His cannons had almost no range at all ... a thousand yards, at the most. He'd have to settle for the last few.

Fyfe caught the ascending line of Boomerangs right as the last few passed the sixty-thousand foot mark. He started with the third from the end and went down the line, all six cannons pumping shells into the strange, black craft. The third from the end caught several dozen rounds squarely in the nose and blew up. Fyfe cried out in joy, not noticing that when the enemy exploded, the air was filled with droplets of a black fluid.

The second from the end suffered a similar fate. Fyfe was on top of the world. He was into it at last. His heart pounding, he trained his guns on the last ship and pressed the trigger. This burst went off target, though, and caught the alien in the left wing. It spun out of formation, spiraling down toward the ground. Close-in fighting was the Outrider's specialty. In an instant, Fyfe was after the Boomerang, filling the air over Southampton with tracers. In a desperate attempt to escape, the Boomerang dived as far down as it could, then tried to climb back up, a long stream of black fluid escaping the several holes in it. But it clipped the spire of St. William's, cutting a deep gash in the wing and sending it diving for the last time to Earth.

His engines roaring, Fyfe followed the enemy down. Coming in at a shallow angle, it passed over several blocks of flats before crashing in a newly built section of parking lot to the north of Bitterne Stadium. The Boomerang split open when it crashed, but there was no fire. It lay in pieces, spilling great amounts of a viscous black fluid onto the tarmac. The parking lot was curiously devoid of people. No one seemed to be around. Fyfe made two passes over the area and, after reporting what had happened to the tower at New Romney, set his plane down a few hundred yards from the Boomerang. As the wings adjusted to the vertical and the Outrider slid straight down to the pavement, Fyfe felt a sudden foreboding. There was indeed no one around; no spectators attracted by the crash, and no children to cop souvenirs. Of course, it *was* a holiday, but still; there was a game on. At least it looked that way. Apart from where the crash occurred, the stadium lot was filled to capacity with autos.

Fyfe left his helmet in the plane, hopped to the ground and, an instinct working he didn't understand, drew his service automatic.

The Boomerang was laid open by the crash. Inside, several large tanks had ruptured, flooding the pavement with liquid. Trying to ignore the stench, Fyfe walked ankle-deep in it, circling the ship until he was certain the Boomerang was pilotless. "Seems to be a bloody robot tanker," he mused, bending to stick his finger into the liquid covering the ground.

"What's this then?" he asked himself, sniffing the syrupy liquid protein, screwing his face up in revulsion, then wiping his finger on his flight suit.

He stood straight up and looked around. At a distance down the side streets, a number of people were approaching. They looked pale, terrified, unwilling to come anywhere near the scene. Fyfe looked to the stadium. One large entrance ramp was open, but he could see no activity inside.

Holstering his automatic, he walked slowly into the arena.

TWENTY-ONE

"Sixteen thousand and forty-two people," Jenson said, shaking his head in disbelief and holding the computer printout unsteadily in his hand.

"That's the final figure, sir," Leslie replied quietly. "It's taken them two weeks to arrive at it."

"I wish they never had. This is grotesque." He dropped the printout onto the floor of Copernicus Control, where Broadsword kicked at it idly. "If only we could have got some shuttles after them."

"There was only me," Broadsword said, "and we found out about the attack way too late."

Jenson nodded, took a large gulp of air, and bobbed his head in reluctant agreement. "Yes, after what they did to us on H5, we were lucky to get this far. Did you read the full report on the Boomerang Captain Fyfe shot down?"

Broadsword shook his head.

"It was a robot tanker, carrying five thousand gallons of liquid protein."

Broadsword grimaced.

"Yes," Jenson nodded, "that's where it's from.

Our Great Thinkers back on Earth figure that five of the Boomerangs which attacked the stadium were piloted and armed and designed to stun the victims and . . . extract . . . the protein. The other five were robot tankers."

"And since Fyfe knocked down three of them . . ."

"Precisely . . . our alien friends will be back for more, and probably not too far in the future."

"*Armada* must know we tipped off the R.A.F.," Broadsword said. "I think they'll come here first, Admiral . . . do you think these guys are going to stick around as long as there's food for the taking?"

"Probably. It's easier to stay here than go looking for another pasture full of cows which, I'm afraid to say, is how they regard us. Oh, we've been more trouble to them than they imagined. But they know they can get onto Earth, strike, and be out with a few weeks' food in around an hour. There are hundreds, if not thousands of places on the planet which are more than an hour away from atmospheric air cover. Up to now, they've picked populated areas . . . out of hunger, I suppose. Once they've settled into a routine, I would imagine the next target would be an isolated village in Siberia . . . or Malaysia somewhere."

Leslie interrupted. "Earth flight coming in on runway one," she said.

Broadsword chuckled. Throughout it all, NASA pretensions still held. There was only one runway at Copernicus, so numbering it was nothing more than public relations.

Jenson and he watched as, in ordered procession, five Russian and five new American shuttles

190

skidded down the runway and formed up in a line outside the base. Two of them slipped into the two remaining docking bays.

"We should be safe now," Jenson said, with understandable relief.

"As long as you don't let them stay formed up in a neat line like that," Broadsword said, indicating the parked shuttles.

"Right," Jenson agreed, "it's Pearl Harbor all over again. Very good, Captain. I don't know what's happening to me."

"Don't blame yourself, Admiral. It's hard to imagine this chunk of rock and dust as being a military target."

"I'll have to, for a while. Excuse me while I go disassemble that bull's-eye out there."

Broadsword wandered over to an unoccupied pinball machine and fed it with a token. The machine was decorated with color transparencies from the previous year's popular movie about prize fighting. Every time a major point was scored, the pugilist's right fist lit up. Broadsword rolled up points, and even managed to work up an interest in the task, until he felt Leslie's arm around his waist.

"I apologized to Margot," she said.

"Oh. Where did you see her?"

"On my way here. She was heading for the East kitchen. She was trying to figure out how to bake a soufflé in a microwave."

Broadsword laughed. "Margot? Cook? Her idea of cooking is to heat up a frozen pizza, and I'm not even sure she can do that."

"That's what she said," Leslie insisted.

"And a soufflé? We're on the goddam Moon. The

gravity is one-sixth and the air pressure seven-eighths. There's no way you could make a soufflé here."

"Nathaniel..."

"At least it wouldn't be easy. I think she was pulling your chain."

"That's what she said," Leslie said again.

Broadsword finished his pinball game by blowing a simple shot, scowled at the low score and led Leslie toward the exit.

"I've got to find out what this is all about," he said.

Broadsword was walking fast, but Leslie kept up with him. "I don't understand. What's so important about Margot's cooking?"

"I don't know. It intrigues me. What else is there to do, anyway?"

Leslie slipped a hand under the back of his trousers. "I probably could think of something," she said.

Broadsword removed her hand. "Later," he said, and led her down to the kitchen.

The four communal kitchens at Copernicus were each little better than the kitchen in Broadsword's apartment back at H5. Now that they were serving twice the normal number of people, matters were even worse. When Broadsword and Dixon got to the East one, they found Margot sitting drinking a beer, her feet propped up on the table. If she was cooking, it wasn't obvious.

"Hello, children," she said cheerily.

"I'm glad you're feeling better," Broadsword said.

"I'm perfect. I haven't seen Baxter in two weeks,

and couldn't give a shit if I never saw him again. I've been reading this thing."

Margot displayed the instruction manual for the wall-mounted oven. "You know, Broadsword, these things are pretty dangerous. You can cook a hot dog in thirty seconds, and fry your ass in only a bit longer."

"Meaning?"

"Meaning I got the whole mess figured out," she said. "I know how to get rid of that big ship circling this section of space."

"How's that?"

"You remember that Curtiss said there might be a fly in the alien ointment? Well, there is. Microwaves."

"Microwaves," he said, steadily.

"Yeah. Remember Sergei, Baxter's friend? Where was he found?"

"In one of the shafts."

"Just past the main microwave generator," she said.

"Right, now that you mention it."

"And the chick who was the only intact corpse in that town in North Carolina?"

"In the kitchen," Broadsword said, with increasing interest.

"Fiddling with the microwave oven."

"But it wasn't on."

"It shut itself off. They have auto switches. And remember that Boomerang we were chasing? The one that got *Lexington?*"

"It blew up in the microwave beam from Solar Collector One," he exclaimed.

"You got it," Margot said triumphantly.

"But microwaves aren't lethal, at least not in moderate amounts."

"To us. But to them? Broadsword, I think you and me got this thing's Achilles' heel!"

Broadsword patted Margot lovingly on the head. 'You're starting to talk like Curtiss," he said.

Mock anger welled inside her, but was cut short by a hurried announcement on the public address system.

"Red alert, red alert! Enemy fighters approaching this base."

Just as all hell broke loose, Broadsword took off on a run for the dome.

TWENTY-TWO

Laser pulses were everywhere. They glanced off the slippery glass of the dome and hit the ground, kicking up puffs of Moon dust. The sky seemed alive with Boomerangs. From the missile emplacements on the rim of the base, Rock Busters soared off tracers into space, one of them occasionally connecting to turn a Boomerang into splinters of metal. Broadsword ran through the dome and up the spiral staircase, with Leslie right on his heels.

The gunner who'd greeted them after the H5 evacuation was at the radio, frantically trying to help the fleet of new shuttles get off the ground. On seeing Leslie, he jumped out of the seat, giving it over to her.

"You do it! The only ones who'd gotten clear of that tight formation they parked in are *Sevastopol, Potemkin, Midway, Coral Sea* and ... shit ... that one that means October Revolution!"

"*Oktyabrskaya Revolutsia,*" Leslie said, taking the controls.

Broadsword looked out at the sad scene as five of the ten new shuttles scrambled toward the runway against impossible odds. The five spacecraft they flew into Copernicus with had been destroyed on the ground.

"How the hell did this happen?" he spat.

"Sunrise on the Moon. They came in over the horizon...low...just when the solar wind was obscuring the sensors."

"Jesus! Why didn't anybody think of that?"

"I don't know! I'm a goddam gunner! And I got to get to my station!"

The man ran down the stairs. *Sevastopol* and *Potemkin* were on the runway, trying desperately to take off, racing down the dusty strip toward the mountains. Laser pulses caught them at the halfway point. They blew up, showering the moonscape with debris. "Damn," Broadsword swore, and jumped up the ladder leading to the turret.

Jenson was in the gunner's seat, slumped over dead. Broadsword stared at him. His heart, no doubt, Broadsword thought. The turret was intact. Broadsword eased the body onto the floor, replaced it and opened fire. The number of Boomerangs seemed to be infinite; in fact, there were twenty, all the aliens deemed necessary to knock out the one thing that stood between them and dominance of the space surrounding Earth. The gunners on the crater rim got six before they were blown away. The rim gunners at Copernicus had accounted for eight. Broadsword got one with his second salvo.

Five remained. The two remaining rim gunners concentrated their fire on another, and got him, just as he swept in for another pass. The salvos were their last. Two Boomerangs opened fire from the southwest and hit them, severing their vacuum hatches and sucking them out into space to float forever, bloated and grotesque. One of them was the man to whom Broadsword had spoken just a few moments earlier.

The four remaining enemy fighters formed up in two rows and came in at a low angle. Broadsword pressed his eye against the target frame and held the trigger down. The Russian deuterium fluoride laser went into its rapid fire sequence. It hissed and growled as gas poured into the chamber and gears protested the twisting of the turret. For a time all was flame and brilliance, then two Boomerangs vanished in plumes of fire. For a split second, Broadsword exulted. It nearly killed him.

For in the time it took for him to smile, laser pulses from the two remaining Boomerangs hit the turret squarely and with considerable force. Broadsword yelled as the deuterium fluoride glowed, then started to detonate. Instinctively, he used the same maneuver he'd used dozens of times to get out of the cockpit of the *Ark Royal*. He dived backwards, curling in the semigravity and slipping headfirst through the hatch leading to the radio room. As he did so, the laser turret blew up and shattered the top of the dome, depressurizing the gun emplacement and causing the vacuum hatch between it and the radio room to slam shut with a loud clang of steel.

Broadsword fell to the steel plate floor of Copernicus Control at Leslie's feet. She cried out in fear and helped him up.

"They're all gone! All the shuttles! They got

them right on the ground! All our guns are gone! We haven't a chance!"

Broadsword looked at the destruction around him. The base was cut to bits, sliced like a round of Edam cheese. Smoke poured out of a dozen breaches, and armor plates lay scattered like clam shells on the Moon dust. The two remaining Boomerangs hung in space less than an eighth of a mile from the dome. Broadsword never imagined anything with such a beautiful shape could be so ugly. They were cruel slits in the Universe, come to get him. He didn't know what to do. He could only remember half of the Lord's Prayer, and mouthing it seemed pointless anyway. He stood still, holding Leslie to him, awaiting death.

The Boomerangs moved closer. The cockpits were apparent then, cruel black triangles. Broadsword wondered if they were fighters or tankers. Would he finish his life a casualty of war or just a spoils of it; a few ounces of liquid protein to be consumed by a race which had nothing better to do than prowl the galaxy, extinguishing life? Broadsword thought of these things, but Leslie saw salvation. The bright white light came from behind the enemy fighters, moving with unimaginable speed.

As it grew nearer, they could make out the flared wings, the round, fat body, and the rust spots. *Columbia* came from over the crater wall and opened fire at seven miles, the Rock Busters searching through space like avengers. Broadsword's eyes were blazing as the missiles struck home, fragmenting the last two enemy fighters.

When the fires died away and their eyes adjusted, the radio crackled with a Kentucky accent

Broadsword had long known and missed a great deal.

"Hey, boy . . . you there?" Baxter asked.

Exeter had made it out of bay 1 and part of the way down the taxiway before being destroyed, so Baxter pulled the *Columbia* into her dock. Broadsword was there to meet him and they embraced, standing amid the smoking rubble. Coughing, her face marred with soot and ash, Leslie stood nearby, shaken and frightened.

"How you doing, Broadsword?" Baxter growled happily. "I was wondering if you were still alive."

"Just barely. Where were you? We were all worried."

"It's a long story, but the upshot is I'm here, and none too soon from the looks of it."

Broadsword put his arm around Leslie, and the three of them started slowly through what remained of the base. Two-thirds of the rim had decompressed, and four of the five bays were out of operation. Three spokes were sliced open, and pieces of vacuum glass and metal plates lay everywhere. Slowly, stunned, the survivors of the colony picked their way out of the blastproof mine shafts.

"This here's some mess," Baxter said.

Broadsword nodded. "It would have been worse if you hadn't shown up."

"I almost didn't. Those two Boomerangs I was chasin' when you saw me last were playin' me for the same sucker they played *Lexington*. Drawin' me off so's a couple of their buddies could sneak up behind me. I got 'em, all right, but one guy behind me shot all the hell out of my right wing thrusters. I barely got away."

"Where'd you go?"

"Way the hell out into space. Once they stopped chasing me, I made a nice, long elliptical orbit for myself, came 'round the other side of Earth and landed on the Moon."

"Where?"

"Right where no one would think to look for me—the Apollo 11 Monument."

Broadsword smiled. "Goddam tourist," he said.

"Yeah, well I fixed up the thruster in a couple of days and was givin' serious thought to coming to find you."

"Why didn't you?"

"I kinda felt you'd need an ace up your sleeve, even if you didn't know it was there. So I parked my carcass on Piazza Smyth, up in the Sea of Rains to the north of here, and waited for the fun to start."

"Jesus," Broadsword breathed, "you sure cut it close."

"You knockin' me, boy? If so, better count your blessings. How many people we got left here?"

"Around sixty. All the H5 colonists are still with us. We lost all the pilots and gunners, though . . . all the shuttles, even the *Ark Royal*." Broadsword's speech faltered, and a cold chill ran up his spine. In the terror of the attack, he'd completely forgotten. Baxter knew right away what he was thinking about.

"Where is she?" he asked.

"Oh my God!" Leslie exclaimed. "Margot!"

"I . . . I last saw her in the kitchen," Broadsword said. "The red alert sounded, and . . ."

Broadsword started running down the rim section toward the bay where the *Ark Royal* was berthed. Baxter was right with him, and Leslie a short distance behind.

When Broadsword reached the dock, his stomach tightened like a fist. The *Ark Royal* was an utter shambles, cut open by laser fire in the seconds before the vacuum doors closed automatically over her. One wing was cut clean off. Wires and hydraulic lines hung from the wound like intestines. The cargo bay doors were sprung open by some dying convulsion of the hydraulic system, and the entire port wall of the cockpit was blown apart. Margot was strapped into the pilot's seat, blood trickling from a stomach wound.

Leslie screamed. Broadsword leaned through the gaping hole in the fuselage and touched Margot's forehead, brushing aside some strands of hair that, sticky with blood, were matted against her skin.

"Margot?" he whispered.

Slowly, painfully, she opened her eyes.

"I tried to take her up...save the ship for us...I'm sorry."

"Let's get her out of there," Baxter said.

Broadsword nodded, undid the straps and helped lift her from the cockpit and onto the floor of the dock. They laid her down gently, resting her hands by her sides, then knelt to left and right of her.

Grimacing in agony, she focused her eyes on Baxter, and smiled. "I knew you'd come back," she said.

"Curtiss saved all our lives," Broadsword said. "The base, too. He was just in time."

"I knew you hadn't run away." She started to

cough and a drop of blood ran down her cheek. Baxter wiped it away, then grasped her hand.

"Listen, kid," he said, "when you get better, I was kinda thinking... well, maybe it's time for me to get my feet on terra firma again. This livin' in space ain't such a hot idea after all. Maybe you and me could go and take a walk in that woods back at the Cape where Geronimo here likes to hang out."

"Yes," Margot said, "yes." And she squeezed Baxter's hand and died.

Broadsword slumped against the hulk of the *Ark Royal* and stared up at the heavens, tears in his eyes. Baxter joined him, and for a long time the only sound was Leslie's sobbing. That too stopped at last.

"She had this idea . . . just told me about it . . . microwaves. . . ."

"The thought occurred to me, too," Baxter said.

"Solar Collector One," Broadsword said.

Baxter nodded and got to his feet. "I'll warm up *Columbia*. You get yourself a Flex Suit and come along."

He walked off, slowly and sadly, and Broadsword pulled himself to his feet. He took a last, sad look at *Ark Royal*, then helped Leslie up.

"Nathaniel... I'm so sorry."

He smiled grimly. "You run things here for a while. Baxter and I will be away for a while."

TWENTY-THREE

With Baxter at the controls and Broadsword sitting beside him, *Columbia* tore up the dust runway and, ascending the gentle slope of that part of the crater wall, vaulted into space. Behind it was the wreckage of Earth's entire shuttle fleet and a devastated Moon colony in which tired, frightened people huddled in blastproof tunnels against the possibility of a final attack.

Columbia roared at full throttle through space littered with debris. In a sector not far from Copernicus, the hulk of the *Concord* drifted, dead. The great wheel of H5 still spun, but was lifeless, even the artificial daylight having gone out. And everywhere were bits and pieces of spacecraft, some alien and some of Earth manufacture. As *Columbia* moved away from the Moon, the radio came alive with requests for information from an Earth every bit as worried as the stranded colonists at Copernicus.

"*Columbia,* this is Kennedy Control."

"They picked up your transponder signal," Broadsword said.

"I should have shut the goddam thing off. I don't want any publicity for this little trip of ours."

"Then ignore them."

"That's what I intend to do," Baxter replied, shutting off the radio.

"I hope *Armada* hasn't picked us up," Broadsword said. "I've seen enough Boomerangs to last a lifetime."

"And I'm fresh out of Rock Busters. Don't worry, kid. There was only one alien left after that attack on Copernicus, and he wasn't in too good shape."

"One left? I thought we got all of them."

"Nope. There was one shot to shit and trying to limp back to *Armada*. I doubt he made it, though. Probably fell to the Moon's surface and blew up on impact."

"That's too good a fate for the bastards," Broadsword said. "Do you happen to know how to run the controls at Solar Collector One? I never set eyes on them."

"I've seen it done. I was there when they ran the early tests. Between the two of us we'll figure it out."

Columbia sailed on, alone. If *Armada* took notice of her, there was no indication. Only Earth seemed to be watching, and Baxter wasn't listening to anything she had to say. The great panels of Solar Collector One were coming up fast, and Baxter fired the retro-engines. The collector array was like a gigantic butterfly, and alongside it *Columbia* merely a speck. Baxter brought *Colum-*

bia to a smooth landing at SC1s sole bay, and Broadsword activated the docking hatch.

"We made it, kid, let's see if we can run this thing."

Broadsword followed Baxter from the cockpit, through the exit hatch and into the living area of SC1. Resting at the precise juncture of the four solar panels, SC1 Control was little bigger than the old Skylab. It had living quarters for six and provisions for a month, but most of it was taken up by machinery. A room the size of a three-bedroom house held the automatic equipment which took electricity from the solar collectors, converted it into microwaves and beamed it to Earth, to be converted back into electricity by the receiving station in Nebraska. Just outside SC1 Control was a quarter-mile-wide microwave dish aimed at the receiving station.

Baxter sat at the single, functional control panel and punched up a view of midwestern America as seen from the eye of the microwave antenna. Cross hairs were centered on a view of the receiving station 22,300 miles below.

"Now we got to move this goddam antenna, that's all," Baxter said.

"Should be nothing to it," Broadsword replied.

Baxter grunted ironically and peered close-up at the panel. For several long, pregnant seconds he scanned the various buttons, monitors and gauges. "I wish I had a goddam cannonball to fire instead of this thing. Well, here goes nothing."

He pressed two buttons in sequence and machinery off in the distance began to whirr.

"You got it figured out?" Broadsword asked.

"Yeah. Can you ring up Kennedy on this thing?"

"Sure." Broadsword established a radio link with Kennedy Space Center.

"Tell 'em what we're up to."

"Kennedy Control," Broadsword radioed, "this is Broadsword. Respond, Kennedy Control."

"Kennedy Control, please repeat identification."

"This is Broadsword and Baxter."

"What happened, Captain? We can't raise Copernicus Base."

"Enemy attack on Copernicus Base. All shuttles destroyed on ground with the exception of *Columbia*. Most H5 personnel okay, but need craft for evacuation to Earth."

There was silence for a moment, while Baxter kept fiddling with the microwave controls.

"Acknowledged, Broadsword ... two shuttles from Kennedy and one from Soviet Union will be made ready for passengers. What are Baxter and you doing at SC1?"

"That's hard to explain, Kennedy," Broadsword replied. "Watch with us and see what happens. Oh, and tell Nebraska we're gonna turn out the lights for a while."

Not wanting to explain further, Broadsword shut the radio back off. Baxter pushed several more buttons. The beam shut off and the target monitor started to swing to the right. As the two men watched, it swung across America, out of daylight and into darkness as the cross hairs passed the Mississippi, then over the Atlantic and off the eastern limb of Earth and out into space.

"What're the Granny coordinates for *Armada?*" Baxter asked.

Broadsword fished from his pocket the data cassette he'd made en route from Copernicus. He pushed it into the tape player and fed it into the main computer.

"There you are. *Armada*'s distance and trajectory for the next six hours."

"We're only gonna need six minutes, if that."

Baxter punched up the information. The large microwave dish swung more and more to the right, until the image of the alien warship appeared in the cross hairs.

"That's it," Broadsword said.

Baxter moved the dish ever so slightly until the cross hairs centered on a spot one third of the way forward from the transom. "That should be the engine room," Baxter grunted.

Armada sailed on, all turrets and antennas, bristling with guns. It looked quietly ominous, a frightening thing, even in the sterile picture offered by the monitor. "Let's get it over with," Broadsword mumbled.

Baxter shrugged and pressed the button to restart transmission of the microwave beam. As all the power that until recently provided twenty-five percent of America's electricity poured into *Armada*, the alien warship started to glow. A shell of light appeared around it, and Broadsword could see lightning bolts jumping over its skin, from turret to turret, antenna to antenna.

Sound doesn't travel in the vacuum of space, but Broadsword swore he heard a roar like nothing ever imagined. *Armada* blew up in a fireball that blanked out the stars, eliminated darkness from the Earth for a day and a half, and for a week was the brightest object in the sky, apart from the sun and Moon. NASA experts called it the biggest explosion in this corner of the universe since the supernova which ended the age of the dinosaurs seventy million years earlier.

Seven weeks after Haskins first spotted it, *Armada* was gone. When the fires went out, not even a skeleton remained. Pieces of the warship would rain on Earth for weeks afterwards, burning up in the atmosphere to create a spectacular display in the night skies.

As *Columbia* cruised back to Copernicus Base, the fireball had just begun and was blinding. Broadsword was grateful for the electronic navigation at last, because visual flying was nearly impossible. Baxter brought the old spacecraft in over the southeast quadrant navigation beacon and turned to port in the direction of Copernicus. The large crater was one of the most prominent features on the Moon. Finding it was no problem, even with the extraordinary light of the fireball.

Columbia flew slowly over the Sea of Nectar, setting a leisurely pace. The base would be safe indefinitely; withdrawal of the colonists to Earth was merely a precaution. H5 would have to rebuild, and Copernicus was by no means a fitting base from which to do it. Once repaired, Copernicus would resume mining operations and scientific research.

Broadsword and Baxter stayed quiet for most of the trip from SC1 to the Moon. Both were numbed by the events around them. Things had happened far too fast. Broadsword felt both exhausted and relieved. A horrendous episode was over, and all he wanted to do was find Leslie and fall asleep in her arms. He'd sleep for a week, or maybe a month, and for the first time in seven weeks not worry if he'd be alive the day after.

It was Baxter who finally broke the silence. "You think they know what's happened?" he asked.

Broadsword shrugged. "It's hard to say. Leslie put them all in the blastproof tunnels, and there are no radios down there."

"Did she stay up top?"

"She was going to, so she could work on the radio link with Earth. She might have let them out. I don't know."

"You know, Broadsword, when I get to think of it, she's not such a bad girl. I realize Margot never thought too much of her, but Margot was a cynical old broad. She didn't like anything that looked young and fresh. No . . . I mean it, Leslie's not such a bad deal."

"Thanks."

"You gonna marry her or anything like that?"

"What do you want from me, for Christ's sake? I'm not making any plans. Maybe I'll wrap myself around Leslie and hibernate. And what do you care, anyway?"

"Let me put it this way. There's no reason now why we can't get on with workin' my mining claim at Eichstadt. That is, unless you're gonna get yourself married."

"Can we put off this discussion for a couple of weeks?" Broadsword said irritably. "I'm just not in the mood."

Baxter frowned and peered out the windscreen. Copernicus was growing larger in front of them. As it increased in size to fill the windows, Baxter switched the *Columbia* from automatic to manual and grasped the stick firmly.

"I'm just gonna plant her in the same spot as before," Baxter said, and Broadsword nodded.

But as the *Columbia* came up over the rim of the crater, and the two men aboard saw the base laid out in front of them, they got a serious shock.

"Holy shit," Baxter breathed when he saw the angry black Boomerang parked in the Moon dust alongside one of the wrecked docking bays. The enemy fighter was damaged—plates hung loosely from one wing and the tip of another was nearly blown off.

"Goddamn! We *would* have to be all out of Rock Busters," Broadsword said, half in a panic.

"It wouldn't make any difference. That thing ain't goin' nowhere. But I would like to find out what the hell's happened to the guy flyin' it."

Baxter lined *Columbia* up with the runway and started his descent.

"That must be the guy I saw shot all to hell," Baxter said. "I don't know how he managed to land it."

Columbia was coming down on the runway, the skids down, the retros firing to slow her.

"If everybody's down in the tunnels they should be safe," Baxter said.

"Leslie's on top," Broadsword replied grimly. "She was working on the radio."

Baxter nodded. The *Columbia* was on the runway, throwing dust to all sides. "Open the chart box," he said, pointing at that section of the copilot's panel. "I got me an old .45 that I keep in there. Never did get around to usin' it. Maybe the time's come."

Baxter brought *Columbia* to a halt in the docking bay vacated by the doomed *Exeter*. Broadsword got the exit hatch open in record time and, holding the old automatic pistol in front of him, ran down the hallway toward the dome.

There was no sign of the colonists. The access ports to the blastproof tunnels remained closed. Smoke still streamed from smoldering insulation here and there, but the base looked no worse than before. The silence was deadly. Broadsword had expected crowds of grateful colonists; instead there was only burning insulation and silence. He ran to the dome. The room was empty, and there was no sound, save for the far-off voices from a radio whose receiver had been fixed but whose transmitter remained out of operation. Kennedy was calling, to no avail. With Baxter close behind, he vaulted the stairs to the radio shack.

Leslie sat against one wall, her knees drawn up to her chin, her eyes paralyzed with fear. The alien was propped against the other wall, his helmet off, blue green blood pouring from a leg wound. He was tall, about six feet, two inches; humanoid; with exaggerated features and pasty white skin covered all over with fine, black hairs. The hair on his head was short-cropped and looked like a skullcap. As Broadsword and Baxter stood over him, he moved his head slowly in their direction, even the eyeballs turning with haughty torpor. Broadsword thought he recognized a fatalistic smirk.

He handed the .45 to Baxter and helped Leslie

to her feet. She hugged him, nuzzled her lips against his cheek, and whispered that she loved him.

"We got *Armada*," Broadsword said.

"I know. I saw it, and heard the messages from Kennedy."

"Does *he* know?" Baxter asked, indicating the alien.

"He hasn't said anything, but I think so. He landed a few minutes after the explosion."

"He knows," Broadsword said. "He's here to give himself up. Probably thinks he can get off the hook in exchange for telling us about their technology."

"I wouldn't be surprised," Baxter replied, with disgust.

"He tapped on the floor with his finger," Leslie said. "It's some kind of binary code, I think. I couldn't make it out."

Broadsword sighed, bent over the alien's leg and inspected the wound. "We can patch this up without too much trouble," he said.

TWENTY-FOUR

The Institute for Space Medicine was housed in the new complex just north of the vertical assembly building. It filled the top floor of the sweeping structure, its huge tinted windows making it resemble a New York City corporate headquarters more than a research hospital. But it was at the Institute that all pre- and post-flight checks of pilots, copilots and passengers were done. Research on the effects of long-term weightlessness was carried out, and doctors routinely subjected Moon miners and H5 researchers to rigorous examinations at the end of their tours of duty in space. The doctors were overjoyed at the return of Curtiss Baxter. Before they got their hands on him, the longest anyone had been in space nonstop was a year and a half.

Baxter took the indignity of being treated as a guinea pig manfully. He hated it, but was determined to prove there was nothing wrong with him despite his decade-long sojourn in planetary space. In fact, he turned out to be in better shape than most of the researchers. Leslie was happy to hear it, but Broadsword and Baxter remained silent. There was too little reason for joy. Everything they cherished had been altered, perhaps forever. Margot was gone, and irreplaceable. H5 wouldn't be rebuilt for years, and Broadsword didn't want to go back there anyway. There were too many memories. *Ark Royal* was a pile of junk lying in the dust of Copernicus Crater, and NASA was balking at spending the money to fire *Columbia* back into space. So there was no ship for him to go anywhere in. To add the final insult, the alien they'd brought down from Copernicus was in the Institute, living in what they regarded as high luxury, with researchers poking, prodding and asking questions but generally treating the creature that might have fired the shot that killed Margot as a celebrity.

Broadsword and Baxter were international heroes, but it didn't make them feel any better.

"We never should have taken him alive," Baxter growled the minute he was discharged from the Institute.

Broadsword nodded in agreement. "You want to get some coffee?" he asked.

"No. I want to get the hell off this rock again."

"Me too," Broadsword replied, with no reluctance.

"They say that blue green blood of his is pretty much like ours," Baxter said. "They also tell me that all in all he's more or less the same as we are. Some things are rearranged or colored differently, but that's it."

"Can't we find something else to talk about?

Let's get some fishing tackle and go down to the beach."

Baxter turned on his young friend, his eyes ablaze. 'Fishing tackle! Jesus Christ, boy, will you ever grow up? You know why they won't put the *Columbia* back into space, don't you? They want us to stump for the goddam budget! It's gonna cost 'em an arm and a leg and both balls to rebuild H5. They want you and me to go to shopping centers and sign autographs. So don't think about fishing tackle ... think of a way to get us off this goddam planet!"

Broadsword knew what Baxter said was true. He wracked his brain for an answer, and was about to confess to inability to find one, when Doctor Haskins came down the hall, as excited as he was when he first spotted *Armada*.

"I was hoping you'd still be here," he said.

"We're on the way out," Baxter snapped.

"Not yet! We've broken through with him. The binary people have a language worked out. He presses buttons and words appear on a monitor."

"Apes did that thirty years ago," Broadsword said.

"Well, it's the best we can do, so far anyway. He refuses to speak, and we're not even sure that he can."

"He just lies there, smirking and pressing buttons, right?" Baxter asked.

"Essentially, yes," Haskins admitted.

"What do you say, Broadsword? You think we ought to talk to him?"

"Only shits smirk," Broadsword said.

"Don't be cynical, boy."

"We thought it was only right for you two to be

215

the first to talk to him," Haskins said. "After all, you caught him."

"Do you want us to apologize?" Broadsword asked.

"No, of course not. We just...well, we want to take your pictures talking to him."

"What did I tell you?" Baxter said, with a bitter laugh. "Come on, let's do it."

Broadsword and Baxter followed Haskins down the corridor and around a corner into a high-security area. They went through two sets of automatic sliding doors manned by armed guards and a nursing station before being admitted to a large hospital room with a spectacular view of the Atlantic Ocean. Breakers swept onto white sands and, in the foreground, a shuttle was being transported to pad 39A.

The alien was propped up on pillows in a large bed by the window. He wore a white dressing gown with the initials of the Institute for Space Medicine on the breast pocket, and was smirking as always. Around him were a passel of technicians and two photographers.

He had on his lap a device the size of a small typewriter, with keys and a personal monitor. It was attached by cable to a large console near the bed at which sat a technician working a larger keyboard with a full-sized monitor. Whenever the alien typed something, it appeared on both monitors in binary symbols and English.

Broadsword felt his stomach turn. The alien was a flesh-eater. He'd helped savage twenty-thousand people, and might have killed Margot himself. To treat him as an honored guest seemed as much an atrocity as the ones he'd committed.

Broadsword wanted to steal the shuttle outside and fly off, never to return. Abruptly, he understood why Baxter so hated his home planet.

"Talk to him, Captain," Haskins said, urging Broadsword toward the bed.

"No," Broadsword said sharply.

"Oh, come on, Captain . . . how hard could it be?"

"I'll talk to him," Baxter said, sidling up to the bedside and staring down at his enemy. "Tell me this, buster . . . how'd it feel to murder the woman I loved?"

Haskins looked stricken, and the man at the console shocked. "I can't ask him that," the man said, and refused to touch the buttons that would do it.

Immediately, Broadsword was on the other side of the bed.

"Where are you from?" he asked.

Haskins grinned. Broadsword, at least, was cooperating. The technician put the question to the alien, who punched some keys. On the screen there appeared the words "far away."

"Why did you come here?" Broadsword asked.

The reply came back immediately. "We were hungry," the alien said.

Broadsword's breath caught in his throat and he turned away, to the window. The shuttle had progressed a few more yards on its journey from the Vertical Assembly Building to the launchpad.

It was then that Broadsword heard a thud and a scream, and a mingling of voices. He spun around to see Baxter using the small console to beat the alien's head into a large, bloody mass.

When Broadsword stepped into the detention apartment, he found Baxter lounging on the vinyl

217

sofa, watching an old war movie on television. Three days had passed, hectic days, with as much politics as soul-searching. Baxter, resigned to the thought that life had once more punched him in the balls, was his old, iconoclastic self.

"Sit down and watch the box with me, boy," he said.

"What's on?"

"*The Cruel Sea.* That was when there were good guys and bad guys, and with any luck the good guys won."

"You're still feeling sorry for yourself," Broadsword said.

"Not me. Just convinced I was right all along about this world."

"I won't argue that. But you *are* off the hook."

"What?" Baxter said, sitting up and switching off the set.

"I got you off. You're a free man, starting right now."

"You mean I can leave?"

"This very instant," Broadsword said proudly.

"Then let's get the hell outta here," Baxter said, standing and shoveling personal effects into his pockets. Within a minute, they were out of the building and walking down a footpath toward pad 39A. A shuttle, brand new and sparkling clean, stood proudly on it.

"How'd you do it?" Baxter asked.

"It wasn't all that hard. I just made them realize how it would look if they prosecuted one of the world's number one heroes for killing a thing which had a hand in wiping out so many lives."

"Is that so?"

"And I said something about telling the press

_ow regally they were treating the alien. It didn't take them long to see the light."

"Terrific, kid," Baxter exulted. "Then I'm off scot-free."

Broadsword stopped walking. "Not exactly."

"What's the matter?"

"I had to give them *something*. You're free ... as long as you leave. And I think they mean don't come back."

"Leave ... you mean?"

"That's right, take the *Columbia* and go. She's all fired up on pad 39B. They even put in a new right wing thruster to replace the one you jury-rigged."

Baxter howled in glee and clapped Broadsword on the back hard enough to disjoint a softer man. "That's all I got to offer them? Christ, I accept!"

"There's one more thing. I had to agree too."

"What?"

"They don't want me around either. I might tell stories they wouldn't like. So they've given me a new shuttle—called it the *Ark Royal*, too. That's it on 39A ... a series 600, the finest made."

"All yours?"

"Well ... permanent loan. I'll be the chief pilot of the first Mars Colony. I guess they think that's far enough away. Anyway, Leslie is the new controller up there, so I won't be too lonely."

Baxter grinned. "In other words, they're kickin'. all our butts the hell off this planet."

"That's about the size of it," Broadsword confirmed.

"Well, I don't mind. Mars is almost on top of the Asteroid Belt. It has a decent gravity, and with those winds they got it won't be too difficult landing. Shit, I can probably stake out a pretty good claim there, in addition to goin' to the Belt all the time. You and me can get our partnership off the ground."

"Considering they're just starting construction on Mars Colony, I guess I'll have a little free time," Broadsword said. "Poking around asteroids with you can't be any worse than what we've been doing."

"Boy . . . I'm gonna make you a rich man," Baxter said, helping himself to a seat on the grass beneath a maple.

"Why not?" Broadsword laughed.

Baxter lit a cigar, and Broadsword slipped to the ground next to him. Behind a row of trees, the new *Ark Royal* shone in the morning sun, and even the *Columbia* a bit further away looked regal.

The two friends lapsed into a silence which lasted until Baxter finished his cigar and stubbed it out in the dirt.

"She told me about the two of you out in the woods there," Baxter said quietly.

Broadsword looked down at the grass, but said nothing.

"Hell, I don't mind. I kind of appreciate your finally gettin' the sense to be turned on by her. I just don't know why it took you so long."

"It just happened. I was a bit crazy and it happened."

"Now, don't minimize it. It was important to her. She loved you, in her own ornery way. Of course," Baxter said with a grin, "she loved me more."

Broadsword picked up a pebble and tossed it at a dandelion growing a few yards away.

"I miss her," he said.

Baxter got to his feet and gave Broadsword a hand up. "Me too, boy," he said, "me too. Come on, let's go have a look at this new steed of yours."

Together, they walked on down the path.

ABOUT THE AUTHOR

Michael Jahn is a popular journalist and novelist whose mystery *The Quark Maneuver* won an Edgar Award in 1978. He has written in many fictional genres, including suspense (*Killer On The Heights*) and historical saga (*Kingsley's Empire*). *Armada* is his first work of science fiction. Mr. Jahn, who lives in New York, is also a long-time contributor to *The New York Times*.